who you think i am

who
you think
i am

CAMILLE LAURENS

Translated from the French by
ADRIANA HUNTER

Other Press
New York

Production editor: Yvonne E. Cárdenas
Text designer: Julie Fry
This book was set in Adobe Garamond by
Alpha Design & Composition of Pittsfield, NH

10 9 8 7 6 5 4 3 2 1

LIBRARY OF CONGRESS CATALOGING-IN-PUBLICATION DATA

Names: Laurens, Camille, author.
Title: Who you think I am / Camille Laurens ; translated from the French by
    Adriana Hunter.
Other titles: Celle que vous croyez. English
Description: New York : Other Press, 2017. | "Originally published in France as
    Celle que vous croyez by Éditions Gallimard, Paris, in 2016" — Verso title page.
Identifiers: LCCN 2016036970 (print) | LCCN 2016047623 (ebook) | ISBN
    9781590518328 (paperback) | ISBN 9781590518335 (e-book)
Subjects: LCSH: Middle-aged women—Fiction. | Self-presentation—
    Fiction. | Identity (Psychology)—Fiction. | Virtual reality—Fiction. |
    Psychological fiction. | BISAC: FICTION / Contemporary Women. |
    FICTION / Psychological. | FICTION / Literary.
Classification: LCC PQ2672.A78365 C4513 2017 (print) | LCC PQ2672.
    A78365 (ebook) | DDC 843/.914—dc23
LC record available at https://lccn.loc.gov/2016036970

prologue

I'd been talking to him for twenty minutes he was saying
something about an article I'd written he'd written a piece
on the same subject I kind of liked his green eyes his black
hair I felt like burying my way into that black hair there
were white patches on the sides grayish-white hairs burying myself in it burrowing my whole face in there touching
it feeling how thick it was smelling it and then his voice
suddenly changed it became really gentle it sounded so tender laden with smoothness or with smooth attentiveness he
was replying to yes to a student she came in to ask him a
question a young brunette with a pink scarf she asked him
something and he turned his back to me just like that without a word with no apology I no longer existed just like that
without a would you excuse me a could I have a minute I
was left on my own idiotic useless no apology with my smile
left dangling I could see it I could see my mouth smiling my
stupid red mouth they look at their teeth like with horses
they prod their breasts and asses you do know they hanged
that woman she'd killed the man who raped her they hanged
her they're killing us it's pure hate you know it's pure hate
listen it was in the paper I cut it out listen look I've pinned
it to my coat there can you see:

3

The rates are written on a notice posted up near the entrance to markets: Little girl aged 1–9: 200,000 dinars ($153) Girl aged 10–20: 150,000 dinars ($116) Woman aged 20–30: 100,000 dinars ($77) Woman aged 30–40: 75,000 dinars ($58) Woman aged 40–50: 50,000 dinars ($39)

Trading in women they sell them but read what it says:

men laughing... amused buyers... Women over the age of 50 are not marketed, as they are unfit for purpose. Besides, the price would not justify the cost of feeding them and transporting them to the market from wherever they were captured. The lucky ones converted to Islam, the rest, the majority, had their throats slit

no I won't calm down they sell us they kill us they liquidate us it's all in the newspaper it depends what sort of paper you read you're men too it's your job it's your hit so then they say that minister Macron it's gross his wife is twenty years older than him everyone laughs about it you really have to be lame a loser a wimp or maybe she's a pedophile people say it's disgusting what a shocking relationship women giggle about it too they laugh about their own impending death these women they're the living dead a few more corpses they don't realize they even kill us the minute we're born and not just in China and India here when you're born "What is it? It's a girl" and you're suddenly worthless Moscovici has a wife thirty years his junior "Beauty and the Minister" run the headlines in the papers while with Macron it's "The Seducer of Crones" no one loves us no one it's horrible you can see it in the street you can feel it you're old people look right through me or criticize me get out of here you stink of death you smell moldy have you seen Madonna people hate her for "still wanting to be someone" that's it those are the very words I read in the paper a real newspaper a serious daily "it's pathetic that aged 50 Madonna still wants to be someone" what should we be doing then should we want to stop existing altogether should we withdraw from who we are accept we don't belong here anymore there isn't room for us there isn't room for me now I don't know where to put myself a drawer a coffin get in your box there's no point being young if you're not pretty and no point being pretty if you're not young men mature women age a man in the twilight of his life is a handsome thing a woman's just sad let them put you in a coffin so transparent I'm transparent my father's a glazer you need to disappear okay get it scram you're in the way get out of my face go die someplace

I

go die!

Go, cruel heart, go die, you never loved me!

— PIERRE CORNEILLE

In some cases when a love cannot happen
it consumes the soul.

— PASAL QUIGNARD

INTERVIEWS WITH DR. MARC B.

Claire

I've already told the whole story ten times to the people you
work with, you could just read my file.

I know you're new, I can see that for myself. Is this your
first job? Because you must be only thirty, at the very most.

You don't look it.

I'm laughing because here I am reciting Marivaux to you
and you have no idea. Have they still not put literature on
the curriculum in this place?

You can tell from, I don't know, the rhythm, the intonation. It's your job to hear how things sound. To spot anything that doesn't ring true. Ding dong. Cuckoo! Hmm,
yes, completely cuckoo.

Araminte. The beautiful widow. And we don't know
whether her young steward wants to seduce her because he
loves her or because she's rich. Whether he's sincere even
though he's manipulating her. But you're no Dorante, I'm
guessing you're not here because you have any plans to
marry me?

I've done a bit of acting, yes, in my day — it was a long
time ago. My husband was a director — well, is. *He* carried

on. We were students when we met, we were in the university theater group. It seems such a long time ago. And yet, d'you know, I still remember some of my lines by heart. I've also learned a bit about staging a performance, haven't I? But let's not go back to the flood of tears. Anyway, it's all been written up in there, in your paperwork. What more do you want?

You need to understand? Oh, I understand *that*! But what exactly do you want to understand?

Well, that's a hell of an answer. You score a point. What's your name?

Marc. Marc. I like you, Marc, and I agree with you: there are only two interesting people in each of us, the one who wants to kill and the one who wants to die. They're not equally well represented, but when you've identified them both you can say you've gotten to know someone. It's often too late.

How did we end up here? We? Kind of you to include yourself in this disaster, when you've only just turned up. No one can blame you for the situation I'm in, I've "ended up in," if I can actually be said to have moved in the last two, um, three years—is it two and a half years?—that I've been here. Or maybe when you say "we" you mean a more general they-we-you? *Us* all? *We,* the institution. *We,* the specialists. *We,* society. How did *we* manage to get into a situation where this woman here present is still living at public expense, where she hasn't accepted her duties, her obligations, her productivity, or should that be reproductivity? So that in her later years she'll be fed, housed, cared for, and given medical care by us rather than doing what she's certainly still capable of doing for the community? Where did *we* fuck up? Is that your question?

I taught. Pretty taut I got too, sometimes.

At university, yes, comparative literature. Senior lecturer. I was about to get my professorship. This they-we-you of yours were about to promote me, to allow me into the wonderful world of mandarins. At forty-seven, they-we-you could say that I was a role model for women, you know there's still a ridiculously low proportion of women in higher positions. And then bang! What a drag! *They* lock me up, *they* cross-examine me, and, till now, *they* keep me here. Will you keep me here, Marc? Will you keep me near you? I'm useless here, I'm not making my contribution to society. I'm deceased in the purest sense of the word, I've ceased to be. Yes, that's it, I'm no longer operational, I've blown a fuse, if you like, or blown a gasket, tripped a switch, and *whee!* I've spun out of control, I'm effectively dead and it's your job to resuscitate me, to rewire my circuits, get the machine working again and basically reinstate me. That *is* what you do, isn't it? — reinstate people. You want the deceased to function again. Which reminds me, there's something I wanted to tell you: you summoned me this mor— What is it? You don't like "summoned"? Okay. You invited me here this morning, it's eleven o'clock, I'm telling you that for future reference, if there is to be any future reference, I'm not really a morning person, not very operational, I can't get up, I'm knocked out by the Valium from the previous evening, and not yet soothed by the daily Xanax, and anyway quite often (this is a secret, don't tell anyone), quite often I don't take it,

I'd rather be anxious than oblivious, if you're unhappy it's better to know you are, wouldn't you say?

In the early days it had nothing to do with Chris—with Christophe—because I'm guessing it's Christophe you want me to talk about? The *corpus delicti* or rather the corpus so absolutely delectable he broke my heart. Or would you prefer me to talk about my childhood, my parents, my family—the whole shebang?

It wasn't Chris I was trying to get to at all, at first. I didn't know him, I wasn't interested in him. I asked him to be my friend on Facebook just to have news of Joe—Joel. I was going out with Joel, with Joe, at the time. In those days Joe had hardly any friends on social networks, he only accepted people he knew, except me—he thought lovers shouldn't be friends. But Chris (and it was Joe who told me this), well, Chris had hundreds of friends, he did a lot of Facebooking, his profile name was KissChris, he had this way of collecting likes so easily it impressed Joe. Are you on Facebook, Marc? You do understand what I'm talking about? You don't need me to translate?

Anyone who's been around Joe for a while might think it was weird for him to be shy like that because in other ways he had no boundaries, I mean really none—hardly even the one that would stop you killing someone outright if you got the urge, and even then . . . there are so many ways of killing someone. He could destroy you in a flash, with one word, with his silence. You must know that women's main fear is abandonment? Yes, you have stuff like that in your books. Well, Joe was like that—I guess you could say "perverse":

he could abandon you ten times a day. He knew where the crack in your armor was—in a way, perverts know women best of all—and he would wedge the tip of his absence in there and just drain your vital energy, your thirst for happiness. You could reach out your hand to him, he'd squeeze it then drop it, on a whim, for no apparent reason, just because you were relying on him, you were relaxing into a feeling of trust. Toward the end I stopped telling him what I liked, I didn't let him know what made me happy because he would have gone to considerable lengths to avoid it or to make sure it didn't happen. When I couldn't take any more I'd leave him, but I never got out completely. And he'd come back all sugary sweet or I'd call him back all honeyed words and the cycle started again, month after month. Don't ask me why. I'd just separated from my husband, I didn't want to be alone, I needed love, or at least to make love, to talk about it, believe in it, well, you must know that song, everyone wants to live, do we need to say why?

No, never. Joe never hurt me physically. It wasn't worth it. Physical cruelty's a last resort, thumping someone in the face is for beginners.

Hard to say. Desire works in mysterious ways. You want something from the other person that you yourself don't have or no longer have. Before I would have said you always want the same thing—a good deep-seated thing from the past, even if it's harmful. Rekindling heartache. Refueling the flamethrower. But since this relationship, I'm not so sure. I've come to think desire might be able to change, that you could uproot it, plant it into new, softer, more accommodating soil. At least try. If everything's written in advance, that would be too sad, I thought. If the die is cast what's the point trying to change the numbers?

Yes. So it was during one of our long breaks, I just couldn't take not knowing where Joe was any longer—because he could vanish, completely vanish—I set up a fake Facebook profile. Till then I'd hardly used it, I had a profile with my real name, Claire Millecam, it was for work, I exchanged information with foreign academics or former students, every now and then, no great shakes. Then I fell into the trap. For people like me who are terrified of being abandoned—that's what you've got written there, haven't you, terrified of being abandoned? Basically a bit like a food allergy: too much abandonment and I'm heading for ana-phylactic shock, I suffocate and die—for people like me the Internet is the shipwreck as well as the life raft: you drown in the tracking game, in the expectation, you can't grieve for a relationship, however dead it may be, and at the same time you're hovering above it in a virtual world, clinging to fake information that pops up all over the Web, and instead of falling apart you go online. If only for that little green light that tells you the other person's online. Ah, that little green light, what a comfort! I remember that. Even if the other person ignores you, you know where they are: he's there on your screen, he's sort of grounded in time and space. Espe-cially if next to the green light it says "Web": then you can imagine him at home, sitting at his computer, you have a mooring in the wild sea of possibilities. What makes you more anxious is when the green light says "mobile." Mobile, don't you see?! Mobile means on the move, roaming, *free*! By definition, harder to situate. He could be anywhere with his phone. Still, you know what he's doing, or at least you feel you do—and this creates a sort of proximity which has a calming effect. You reckon that if he was enjoying what he was doing he wouldn't be going online every ten minutes. Maybe he's watching you too, hiding behind the wall and watching what you're doing? Kids spying on each other. You listen to the same songs as him, almost in real time, you live together through music, you even dance to the same songs that get him tapping his feet. And when he's not there, you have a record of when he was last online. You know what time he woke up, for example, because looking at his wall seems to be the first thing he does. At what point in the day he laid eyes on a photo he commented on. Whether he woke in the middle of the night. He doesn't even need to say so. Basically, you're stitching this together as you go along: you embroider over the gaps, like darning socks. There's a good reason for calling it the Web. One minute you're a spider, the next you're a fly. But you exist for each other, thanks to each other, connected by a shared religion. Not exactly taking communion, but communing.

Of course it hurts too, of course it does: the other person's online, but not with you. You can imagine all sorts of things, you *do* imagine all sorts of things, you look at his new friends' profiles—both male and female—looking for a revelation in someone's posts; you decipher the tiniest comment, you keep cutting from one wall to another, you play back the songs he's listened to, read meaning into the lyrics, learn about what he likes, view his photos and videos, keep an eye on his geo-location, the events he's going to, you navigate like a submarine through an ocean of faces and words. Sometimes it takes your breath away, you stand there holding your breath on the edge of this abyss to which you've been relegated. But it's not as painful as knowing nothing, nothing at all, being cut off. "I know where you are": I needed those words in order to live, do you understand? It's like that epitaph on an American's tomb at Père-Lachaise cemetery—I used to love strolling around there. His wife had had this engraved: "Henry, at last I know where you're sleeping tonight." Wonderful, isn't it?! Facebook's a bit like that: okay, so the other person's alive, but he's assigned a location, he's not entirely free, he's on known territory, even if it isn't conquered territory. So that little green light kept me alive like a drip, a lungful of Ventolin, I could breathe easier. And at night it was sometimes my guiding star. I don't have to explain that. It's a statement of fact. I had a bearing in the middle of the desert, a reference point. Without it I'd be dead. D'you understand? Dead.

And you can go ahead and do what the others did, deducing that I had God knows what sort of fusional relationship with my mother, an inability to break away, a castration complex and everything else. But then don't go saying *in the same breath* that I had the means—that I *have* the means—to move on to something else: my work, my friends, my children. I was the child. Okay? I *am* the child. There's no specific age for being a kid. You must have that written somewhere in the file, that I'm the child?

What is a child? How can I put this... It's someone who needs looking after.

It's someone who wants to be cradled.

Even if it's an illusion, yes, why not? It's still just as soothing. Ha, now you're pleased with yourself! Nice line: *even if it's an illusion?* In a smooth voice. Are you a doctor or just a psychologist? Mind you, what's the difference? What I don't like about your discipline, your so-called science, is that it doesn't change anything. However much we understand what's going on, what's gone on, we're still not saved. When we understand what's causing our pain, it still hurts. No benefit. We can't be cured of our failures. You can't darn ripped sheets.

Are you on Facebook, Marc? You're not answering. You're not proud of it. *You* don't stalk people, do you. You get enough from your job.

So anyway, because I couldn't follow Joe directly, I sent Chris, KissChris, a friend request. He was the perfect contact because he'd recently moved into Joe's apartment, although only intermittently. They'd met about ten years earlier in the editorial department of *Le Parisien*, where they both worked, Chris as a photographer, Joe as an intern, they were about twenty-five at the time. I got the impression they did a lot of partying together for two or three years before having a bust-up over work, a girl, some weed, or money. And then, at the time I'm talking about, they'd just reconnected through some other guy who patched things up between them. Chris was struggling, every now and then he'd get some minor reportage, a photo for a scummy magazine, but he mostly lived on benefits. Meanwhile Joe was happily unemployed and about to move into his family's holiday house in Lacanau, near Arcachon—a dreamy place where I had, where I still have, wonderful memories: time passes, the memories remain, as cemeteries say. Because there were good times with Joe. A few. Maybe there are good times with everyone. There can be. His parents inherited a fortune from a childless cousin, money wasn't a problem for him anymore. He vaguely made music—nothing serious—but his mother was keen for him, aged forty, to maintain some semblance of work: so he was the caretaker and the gardener and the plumber and the electrician. Or so to speak, because he couldn't do any of those things. He couldn't bear being on his own and, because I lived in Paris, I couldn't go see him very often (I sometimes think that was the main reason he finally moved out to the country: to make it difficult for me to see him), so he offered to put Chris up. Marguerite Duras wrote something about that, about the fact that men really like being among men, do you see what I mean, there's a sort of laziness, a lack of interest in women—too different, too tiring. Women require an effort that they don't feel like making, not long term anyway. Except for fucking, I guess. They bolster each other with their mutual virility, they don't want a woman inside their heads or right in front of their faces. I imagine Joe was also thinking he could resuscitate his younger days, start over. He could never deal with the idea of growing old. In his own mind he was still eighteen, he fantasized about very young girls, minors, virgins—did you know that the combination of "teen" and "sex" is the most common Google search in the world?—well, basically, he thought you could keep playing the same film over and over. That's what they did, anyway. Chris moved in with Joe, like in the good old days.

I'd never met Chris in the flesh. Joe had told me a few things about him, that was all. I think he didn't want me to meet him: he hid it well but Joe was extremely jealous, he was always frightened of losing what he had, including what he didn't want. If he'd lost something everyone had to lose it, if something was dead as far as he was concerned, it couldn't keep going someplace else. One of the last times I saw Joe in Paris before the meltdown, he just showed me the photos Chris was taking and posting on Facebook to drum up some interest, make a bit of buzz, as he called it. He wasn't very kind about his "best buddy"; according to him, Chris wasn't really looking for a job. He was fed and housed in Lacanau, so why move? Then his ambition was to become famous without lifting a finger—maybe just his index finger to press the start button. "He's hoping someone will notice him one day and turn him into the next Depardon," Joe scoffed. His photos were good, I looked at them in detail, but only because it was a way to spend time with Joe.

Chris? No, I never actually spoke to him, before. Well, yes I did, it came back to me the other night, I had a nightmare and the words came back to me, should I tell you this? You're interested in nightmares? Okay. It was morning, I had a lecture, I went into the amphitheater, all dressed up, nice makeup, I headed for the podium and just then all the seats emptied in a flash, all the people were wearing blue, they got to their feet as a block, clumped noisily down the stairs, and walked out without even glancing in my direction, a thumbs-down, and I was left alone on my platform, an empty platform and not a train in sight. I was frightened, I turned around and there was something written on the board in capitals, in capital punishment, I woke with a start, my heart pounding at a hundred miles an hour, and there were those words, now here you could make a note, get your pen, this won't be in the file. No? Don't you have to write everything down, even tiny details? Aha, listening! Big Brother's listening! Well, the dream reminded me of something in real life. One evening I called Joe in Lacanau, I often did to keep things going—keep our love going, what was left of it. He mostly didn't answer but that evening he did. He'd been drinking or smoking, both probably, either way he was hazy and aggressive, he complained I was checking up on him, calling him only to be sure he was there, to monitor him. And then—and this is something he did if he was bored with a conversation, sometimes in the middle of the street with a random passerby—he handed me to someone else without any warning. Suddenly, in the middle of a sentence I heard a different voice, an unfamiliar voice saying hi, then calm down. It was Chris, I realized afterward. I complained, got angry, this habit of Joe's irritated me, even if sometimes it really made me laugh when he stopped complete strangers in the street... But not this time, the guy on the other end wasn't funny, talking to me like we knew each other, his voice slurred and patronizing, Don't you think you're a bit old to be jealous? he said. I got real mad, I asked to speak to Joe again, She's so not cool this chick of yours, he muttered and then said pompously: So you think you can do whatever you like, you think whoever can call at whatever time of day. I'm not just anybody, I retorted. And at least

I'm not squatting, I'm not sponging off him. At that point I heard him take a toke, then he blew out the smoke and before hanging up—without handing me back to Joe—he said: Go die!

Go die.

The killer words.

People throw themselves out of windows for less than that, don't they? Plenty here would. They've been bashed around by so many words they start to wobble.

Go die. GO DIE. Other people's words follow them around like hostile ghosts. People's voices issue instructions they can't escape. Textual harassment, you could say, ha ha! I like word games too, you see. We should get along.

Anyway, all that to explain that there was absolutely no way I could have predicted what happened next. When I set up my fake Facebook page, Chris was just a parasite as far as I was concerned, a rude misogynistic freeloader, an enemy in my shaky relationship with Joe. I wasn't even considering communicating with him, I just wanted this indirect access to news of Joe.

Go die.

That's what I ended up doing when it comes down to it, didn't I?

In the end I did as I was told. I'm not alive here. Is that what you all think? When you're crazy the imperative sounds like an incontrovertible command, doesn't it? Tell me, is that what you all think? A command that can be turned around too. Oh, go on. That can be sent back to the sender. Go die yourself. When you're crazy. When a woman's crazy.

And is that what's written there, that I'm crazy?
Are all women crazy?

Chris's Facebook status publicly proclaimed he was a photographer, so I set up my avatar, cooking up an identity as a
girl passionate about photography. For my profile picture I
used a shot of a dark-haired girl I found on Google, her face
completely hidden by the lens of a Pentax, all you could see
of her was her hair, by flitting through photos of the girls he
was friends with I'd worked out he prefers brunettes. I said
I was twenty-four (twelve years younger than him rather
than twelve years older), that I lived in Paris but traveled
a lot, I stacked all the odds in my favor. Before sending
him a friend request—I wanted to dangle the bait without
arousing his suspicion—I scooped up a few dozen of his
friends, people I didn't know but who were in photography or fashion, people like him, cool, swanky, hip or losers,
pleased with themselves and friends of the human race, in
love with life, as they say. He accepted me right away. He
was even the one to initiate a conversation because I "liked"
one of his photos. It must have been at the start of the year,
January time; we'd broken up around Christmas, Joe and I
had—the holiday season's a vulnerable time, you feel more
lonely when you're alone, Joe would never miss an opportunity like that, he must have dumped me just before New
Year's Eve. So Chris's message made me happy, it was stupid
because it didn't really say anything, "Glad you like my photos, thanks, happy new year. I'm Christophe, Chris to my
friends," he wasn't coming on to me either, just being polite
basically.

But the connection was there. I replied saying I thought his photos were fantastic, that I'd gone to his exhibition the year before on the rue Lepic (I'd seen the flyer on his wall—a few large prints on sale in a bar-gallery place). He asked me whether we'd met at the time, I said no, he wasn't there when I went. Meanwhile I trawled his wall for information about Joe—a picture of him dressed as a garden gnome, a jokey status about "tending his carrot tops on the balcony," stuff like that. I didn't have any direct contact with him at all.

The conversation with Chris developed very naturally. He asked me what I did, whether I lived in the heart of Paris. I invented a job in events management: I organized fashion-related performances, was badly paid, a perennial intern, but I traveled quite a lot and was shaping up my résumé—I was only twenty-four, after all. I lived in Pantin.

The fashion thing was to keep him interested; the traveling to justify the problems (I anticipated) of meeting him in person if he suggested it—I often went away at very short notice, my boss could need me at any time, lucky I was single. How about him? He lived in Lacanau, in a friend's house a couple of minutes from the ocean, real nice (you bet! Oh, the jolt of jealousy when I read that! He'd taken my place, *I* should have been there, with Joe). The pair of them were planning a trip of several months to India, Goa, they were going to film everyday life there, denounce the poverty and injustice. His friend was also hoping to meet some musicians. He himself was planning to write a book. Did he already have a publisher? No, not really. But several were interested.

Obviously I was sneering on the inside: Joe "denouncing" poverty? That would take a bit of empathy and he didn't have any. Other people don't exist in Joe's world, with the odd exception, he only knows emotionless walk-on extras, animals reduced to their basic urges, or things that can be brushed aside with a flick of the hand. But maybe Chris was different? I thought that straightaway, or hoped it: the simple, friendly way he wrote, he was polite, reserved, his messages were gentle, the exact opposite of Joe, to the extent that I completely forgot his "Go die," you see. Still, the thought of Joe being so far away terrified me: Lacanau was close enough to calm my fears, I could picture going there, imagine the distance as the crow flies, but not Goa.

It wasn't long before I was caught up in the game—it wasn't long before it stopped being a game. In the early days I hurried home from college after classes and couldn't wait to get on my computer. "There goes mom the geek!" my eldest son used to say—he was thirteen at the time. I hardly looked at my real Facebook account where I wasn't likely to have much activity, but went straight to my fake profile.

I chose my pseudonym carefully: Claire because I wanted to use my own first name, ironic as that may seem; Antunes because it's foreign and it's the name of a writer. Do you know António Lobo Antunes? Major Portuguese novelist. You should. He trained as a psychiatrist. But he just writes now, I think. I mean, *is* there anything else?

A foreign name so I could "go away" if need be. And seeing as I speak a little Portuguese...and anyway, all that *fado* and *saudade*, I don't know, it suited me. So: Claire Antunes. There's always something inexplicable about a chosen identity, wouldn't you say? Like in a novel. I'm writing a novel, you know. In the writing workshop, here. I don't show it. No one's read it. Except Camille, who runs the workshop, have you met her? I've nearly finished it.

So that was how it started, softly softly. Chris and I messaged each other every two or three days, getting to know each other. Well, I was getting to know him. He was getting to know Claire Antunes, a twenty-four-year-old on a temporary contract, quite shy, not very into Facebook (I had only about thirty friends), who really loved photography, French songs, and travel. He thought I was cool—that was his word, cool, he used it all the time, about anything; and I'd go online late in the evening when he was almost always online—the pleasure of that little green light!—and we started instant messaging. I always wanted to know what Joe was doing so I tried to get Chris to tell me about his life in Lacanau: wasn't he bored in a village that was deserted in winter? What did he do all day? He said that no, he liked the solitude, that the light over the ocean was beautiful, it was cool. And me? Me, I was the opposite, I saw people, was out a lot. Wow, that's cool. It has to be said, it was kind of limited, and pretty boring for me sometimes, without the sexy or cranky or funny edginess of Joe's exchanges. A bit Boy Scout, if you know what I mean. And I'm sure you do. I was careful about what I wrote, I made some spelling mistakes (and it was painful for me, genuinely, it cost me: I don't like to see the language abused. Language is a reflection of my life. When I really want to die I'll be silent). He made a few mistakes, but not too many—the classic ones my students make: loose instead of lose, trouble with there and their, that sort of thing. I learned to use abbreviations, to drop in smileys, English words, a bit of slang. I didn't have to do much research, my kids supplied the material. I had them every other week at the time, my husband and I were doing joint custody, alternate weeks.

Of course I miss them. What a question. But I don't want to see them. I prefer not to.

I flattered him quite a lot, too, because I knew about men, but well. Yes...you haven't noticed? Aha, that's because you're a man! And an analyst too. To think Freud associated narcissism with women! "Women love only themselves" and all that. Okay, maybe he doesn't say it of all women, that's possible, you know your Freud better than I do. Still, he doesn't say it of men. Narcissistic men weren't what Freud was most interested in, were they? Anyway, I meant it when I paid Chris compliments: he was talented, I was just an amateur, I was impressed by his technical mastery as well as his "eye," his ability to capture the moment. He told me he'd teach me, it wasn't very hard, framing was the most important thing. *He'd teach me:* that was his way of suggesting a future together, a someday when our bodies would be side by side IRL—in real life. And the thought made me anxious, tormented me, like anything that's impossible but that you can't quite dismiss. Accepting you can't do something; now that must be what happiness is.

Getting out of shot when the framing's not right. Getting out of the frame.

On the other hand, I'm in the frame here. There are edges here. I'm always in the picture.

You're here to keep me in the picture, is that it, Marc? Or rather to put me back in the picture? And what if I can't handle you in the shot, what do we do then? Really?! And what about rights to the image? That's reciprocal, isn't it? It's like love. You have a right to it but you can retract from it.

So, Chris then. Pretty soon, but very sensitively, he asked for a photo of me because, he said, he needed to see me. Because the face was obscured in my profile picture, he suggested I send him one in a private message because he perfectly understood I might not want to show myself to just anyone. I think he even liked my shyness, the secrecy thrilled him, or moved him perhaps. He wanted a woman all to himself, a privileged connection. Who can blame him? Before asking for a photo of me he'd commented on my profile picture, the one in which you could see only "my" hair. He could imagine the inevitably pretty girl hiding behind the lens, under those raven locks. But he'd rather have proof…

The photo? You mean the second one? No, nothing special, why?

I chose it at random, yes, like the first one. I Googled "pretty brunette" and dozens of cute girls came up in various stages of undress. I chose a respectable one, obviously. That's all. In fact, come to think of it, Chris must actually have waited quite a long time before asking for a picture of me—several months—even though we messaged on Facebook at least three times a week. He must have quite liked imagining me, dreaming about a hidden face. Some guys are like that, there are more and more of them now, aren't there? who prefer imagining than having someone in their arms, but you can't always tell whether they're afraid of being disappoint*ed* or disappoint*ing*.

No, I'm exaggerating. Because I remember that right back in February he left a message to say he was "hitting Paris" for a few days and asking if I'd like to meet for a drink. I told him, because I had to, that I was off to Milan for Fashion Week, shame. I also asked why he was coming to Paris, whether it was for his upcoming trip. He said yes, he and his buddy Joe were leaving soon, they were just arranging the last formalities, passports, vaccinations. He was disappointed not to be meeting me, but it would keep till another time.

No no, nothing. It's just that... you see, an expression like "hitting Paris," for example, the words "hitting Paris" would usually wind me up. But with Chris, even if I noticed it (I couldn't help myself), it gave me a sort of erotic satisfaction, as if our languages—our tongues, ha!—were merging, entering into a tender physical battle. I made a point of calling instead of sending written messages, to avoid alerting him to these differences, but my desire for him was rooted in them, it fed off them. Rather as you can fall in love more quickly with a foreign accent, an unfamiliar intonation. You're a tourist in love, you're trying to find someone different who's from somewhere different, and you find them first through language. By the way, have you met Michel? The fat little bald guy who always has a dictionary under his arm? Apparently he's been here forever. He studies etymology. Hebrew in particular. At lunch yesterday he told us that "amen" means "I believe it." Wonderful, isn't it? We should end all our sentences like that, especially when we talk about love: amen. I love you. Amen.

Okay. Despite the pleasures afforded by what was in fact a fictional connection with Chris—I say fictional but you have to understand there was also some truth in it, it was a real connection, and it did me good—in spite of that, I was still suffering because Joe had lost interest in me. The thought that he was soon leaving without even calling me again was unbearable. So I plucked up my courage or my craziness, whichever you prefer, and the next week I sent him a text. He replied right away, hi you, I'm going on a long trip, if you want one last good time it's midnight tonight at your place. I said yes, I did want.

I hadn't seen him for several months. He was handsome, tanned, sea-salty, excited about his trip, he was already not really there. Joe lives like everyone else, in the moment, but what makes him different from all the rest is that he takes pleasure not from the present itself but from his certainty, in the present, that the future will make him happy. His present is a present, a gift because it's a constant projection toward a heartwarming tomorrow. His present is glorious because it's wall-to-wall with prospects. So when we slept together that evening, I was making love with a ghost; he was already on the beaches of Goa, surrounded by teenagers who saw him as a hero, he was trading precious stones, getting together a trance group that made him famous, becoming a surfing champion, what do I know... that's Joe all over: he lives happily today on things that will never happen. Joe's the opposite of what I was saying earlier: he never faces up to his own inabilities, ever, he's in constant denial of failure, that's why he's not unhappy. He has no doubts, he's a sort of fundamentalist of life. At least this anticipatory enthusiasm kept the more negative waves away from me: I didn't exist either. He just about mentioned, as he closed the door on his way out, that I should go back to my husband. My life—he seemed to think with one last pitying look at my apartment, my books, and my face—my life wouldn't mean much now that his was going to be so wonderful on the far side of the world. Being happy isn't enough, you also need other people to be unhappy: it's a recognized formula.

But what I could get out of his visit had changed, I soon realized that. I still liked making love with Joe but I was thinking about Chris. It was ironic: I'd met Chris in order to have news of Joe, and now I was talking to Joe to get news of Chris. And I learned something that dampened my mood that evening: Chris had a girlfriend, a twenty-year-old already separated from the father of her six-month-old baby. He'd met her on the beach three months earlier, but they didn't see each other much because she lived in Bordeaux and Chris wasn't going to travel all that way to "hear some other guy's baby screaming—not dumb, our boy," Joe said. At least he didn't meet her on Facebook, I thought, as Joe told me the story—I was so thrown that I clung to the tiniest positive detail; I wanted our relationship ("our relationship"!) to be different. But at the same time I couldn't criticize Chris for multitasking on the love front because what we had wasn't love, just friendship—virtual friendship, at that. "How are things, my new friend?" he'd say, or "Lots of love, mystery friend."

The age difference? How do you mean? Oh, between him and me? No, I thought you meant between Chris and his girlfriend, with him being thirty-six and her twenty: a sixteen-year gap, quite something. But of course, that's not what you're interested in. No, what you're asking is whether the age difference between Chris and me — twelve years — was a problem, is that it? If it were the other way around you wouldn't even ask: if I were Chris, aged forty-eight, in love with a thirty-six-year-old woman, it wouldn't matter at all, wouldn't even cross your mind, I'm sure of it, you wouldn't even have picked up on it. You see, right there you have every woman's tragedy, one of our day-to-day tragedies, and you don't even seem aware of it, when this is your job, after all, the human soul is your job. Or perhaps it's because you're young and you think of all mature women as your mother — in which case, you need therapy, Marc.

But while we're on the subject, you men do make me laugh with your Oedipus complex which you serve up in every possible guise. Killing your father to marry your mother? Hah! You need to come up with a different myth to show what really goes on: a man who kills his wife and sleeps with his daughter, now that would be more accurate, much more accurate. There's what I have to say on that subject. But tell me, why should a woman over forty-five gradually withdraw from the living world, rip the thorny prick of desire from her flesh (ah, the prick! Did you hear that, Doctor?), let's say the thorn then, why should women rip out the thorn of desire when men can start over, have more children and reinvent their whole world until they die? The injustice of it consumes us from a very early age; long before we experience it, we intuitively know it's there. There's something unlimited about men (and I don't mean their intelligence), something that doesn't threaten to close down on them, you get a sense of it even with little boys, and sometimes with very old men. I saw Jean-Pierre Mocky on TV the other day, he was boasting that he was still fucking at past eighty, "I can still get it up," he said, leering at the girl next to him, an actor young enough to be his great-granddaughter. And the audience clapped. "I can still get it up, amen." Can you imagine an eighty-year-old woman saying on live TV that she gets wet eyeing up some teenager. How embarrassing that would be. The truth is it's unacceptable. Men, on the other hand... the world belongs to them more than it does to us—time, space, the streets, the city, work, thought, recognition, the future. It's as if there's always another stage for them, a whole different backdrop they can see if they tilt their heads or stand on tiptoe—it's over our heads, quite literally. For example, I personally have never felt I filled a man's whole horizon.

My sons? When they were little, a bit. But they're teenagers now, they're six inches taller than me, so obviously it's all over my head.

No, not my husband, never! It's just... he was so confident he was the only future I had. "Woman is the future of man," yeah, right! You have to be kidding... or maybe in the plural, women. Like milestones along the way. Or millstones...

The difference is all men have a future. Always. A future without us. Men die younger. Maybe. But they live longer. I read somewhere that on dating Web sites the watershed between forty-nine and fifty is an abyss for women, they get swallowed up by it. At forty-nine they get an average of forty visits a week, at fifty they're reduced to three. And yet nothing's changed, they're the same, just a year older. You must know that sketch, I can't remember who did it, about the expiration date on canned food: "best before March 25, 2017." What exactly happens inside that can on the night of March 25? We women are all cans of food. We become unfit for consumption overnight. And if I'd put the truth on my fake Facebook page, used a real photo of me, Chris probably wouldn't have accepted me as a friend. At least he wouldn't have wanted an intimate friendship with a forty-eight-year-old woman.

Of course I can't be sure. I didn't dare go with the truth, and that's what caused the disaster. Instead of laughing in the face of this injustice, instead of defying it, I interiorized it, I submitted myself to it more than any man would. It's too late now.

You're sweet, trying to make it up to me. You're actually digging yourself deeper. I know, I don't look it. I know men can find me attractive. Do *you* find me attractive, Marc? Are you not allowed to say?

Thank you.

Actually, why thank you? Why do I need this?

Why do I give a damn whether people find me attractive?

Oh! At that point I'd been separated from my husband for a year already. I left him just before I met Joe, with no remorse or scruples, I knew he had a replacement woman or would have one soon enough, as he always had, in fact he remarried. You know he's one of those men who "love women," as people say. A nice way of saying he doesn't love a single one. He wanted me to stay with him, though, but I really didn't like his arguments. "You'll age and soon no one will want you," he said. "You still have...what? Two, maybe three good years? Because guys couldn't give a fuck about mature women. And you can write your theses and articles, and go to the gym, you can stay brilliant and trim, it doesn't mean a thing if your license plates don't have the right date. Whereas I'll still be here even when you're ugly, flabby, and wrinkled, and you can thank me for not leaving you." The narcissism of pity, do you know that one? And he was three years older than me! The skin on his chest starting to sag, his pubic hair going gray, his scalp showing through his hair. Because I can do that too, can't I, make him look like a pathetic, aging specimen! But this was about *my* dying light. He was burying me but offering me a first-rate funeral. The apotheosis of hate when the gravedigger expects you to thank him for digging your grave. But I didn't feel like being dead. If he'd said "I love you" I would have stayed. Well, maybe not. What's love without desire? What is it? How do you do it? Tell me that. I didn't want to be dead, that's all, even with pretty flowers on my grave.

There. Do you understand a bit better now? Do you see how a woman in her forties with a professorship (I'm saying that for your statistics, you do have forms to fill in, right?) can end up in a straitjacket in this mess? Just because she didn't want to die?

"Go die": that's what the whole world tells women to do in more or less explicit terms. And incidentally literature echoes the theme. You need only read Houellebecq—you must have read some of his stuff? That makes you the only one...—or Richard Millet: I remember in one of his novels a woman decides to die at forty. Forty: it struck her (or him!) that that was when a woman lost her looks and, *therefore*, might as well commit suicide. And she does it! And here's what's horrific about the book: the narrator, her lover, stands by all through her death throes as if this is somehow inexorable, programmed, as inevitable as his dwindling desire for her. What else could he do but sadly acknowledge her decline—I'm asking you? As for Houellebecq, we've all heard his song. The premature collapse of women's erotic potential is inescapable because "uneducable" men have judged them only by physical criteria "for millennia," whereas women, who are "educated," can be attracted to wealth, power, and intelligence. And why not educate men? Why are we condemned to insignificance by the very people who claim to pity us? Go die, that's the only advice men have for women, when it comes down to it—it has to be said. Go die, scram, make way for the young, make way for men. Women are everlastingly excluded, second-rate human beings.

Aha! The perfect excuse! Is that all you can come up with? Yes, you have every reason to blush. You remind me of what I was told as a child: you eat your supper, think of all the little Biafrans dying of starvation. Yes, okay, YES, OF COURSE, there's worse somewhere else. Let's say it's more or less metaphorical—but sometimes it isn't. Sometimes it's real, go die, a real instruction. I realize that. Do you think that's any comfort to me? That I should be happy to be a *French* woman because women are dying in other countries? But how can I live here when women have their bones broken over there? Did you hear what that guy said, that Hamadache, I'll never forget his name, it's got the word "mad" right there, he said, "Women should be banned." "I've come to this conclusion," that's what he said, "women should be banned." Mind you, we had that here in France too, a guy in the late nineteenth century, in the days of Huysmans and the Goncourt brothers and every flavor of misogynist, a doctor, I don't remember his name, but his professed ambition was to "eradicate the bug with its hair in a bun." It's a more amusing formulation, but it doesn't make me laugh—not at all.

For a long time now I've woken in the night in a muck sweat with a head full of horrible images—girls in Pakistan disfigured by acid attacks, with holes instead of eyes, their flesh deformed or destroyed by male loathing, women raped everywhere in the world, everywhere, and sometimes hanged for this "dishonor," teenage girls with their throats slit, babies destroyed at birth because they're girls. The statistics gnaw at my brain: forty-eight percent of the population is female, and falling steadily, against fifty-two percent male worldwide because we're being killed, one hundred thirty million women excised, one young woman in three a victim of violence over the course of her life. I'm tormented by an unhealthy empathy for my kind, you know. Every night I howl with terror at the thought of being a woman. As I get older my own sex is becoming the cause of my insomnia. When that girl was raped and battered to death on a bus in India right in front of her boyfriend, I couldn't get her out of my head for days—I could almost say "out of my memory"—the iron rod her attackers used to butcher her insides. I clamped my legs together at night in terror as I thought about it, I pictured the to-and-fro action they must have used to break her open, and the point when they threw her out of the bus like a garbage bag, and I went over and over the words one of them said after he was arrested: "We'd decided to kill a woman." Not to have a good time, to fuck, to have a laugh. No: to kill a woman. Those words fill me with such disbelief, I can't even describe it. I said them out loud in the dark in my bedroom and just couldn't understand. It's like the photos of the prostitutes killed in a brothel in Baghdad, twenty-nine women covered in blood, their heads between their knees as if to protect themselves from the attacker's weapons with whatever pitiful means they had. It just hits me in the face and I have to stifle the sobs in my chest at the sheer tragedy of being a woman. You can go ahead and cite counterexamples like Doctor I-don't-know-what-his-name-was, tell me pretty stories, Marie Curie, Marguerite Yourcenar, Catherine Deneuve, poor guy, he wracked his brains, found it hard, of course he did, you can't get away from the truth: it's a tragedy being a woman. Wherever you are. Always. Everywhere. It's a fight, if you like. But because we lose it's a tragedy. That's why I hardly watch TV anymore, not the news anyway, I've stopped reading newspapers and magazines because I can't bear to see myself treated like that, me as seen through all those women, all those victims. Women are condemned—by force or by contempt—to die. That's a fact, everywhere, all the time: men teach women to die. From north to south, fundamentalist or pornographic, it's the sole same tyranny. Existing only in their eyes, and dying when they close their eyes. And they do close their eyes, and you close your eyes too. You close your eyes to women's fate. Obviously for us there isn't the same level of violence, obviously. We don't die of it, or not so much. That's a hell of a step in the right direction, isn't it? And I got lucky, very lucky even, it wouldn't be right to complain, but that doesn't bother me, I'm doing it anyway. I'm lodging a complaint, flagging up my demise. Have my death recorded, even if it's just in "other news." Because dying in your own lifetime is still an ordeal. You melt into the background, you become a silhouette, a nothing. Let me say it, at least, please, let me, listen to me. Indifference is another form of burqa—does that shock you?—another way for men to corner the market on desire. Another way to close their eyes. We've served our purpose, we're no longer needed. Yesterday's fantasy, today's phantom. Do you think the comparison's inappropriate? Well, I'm not exactly appropriate here myself. Here or anywhere else. I don't belong anyplace. Do you know this one? "What supernatural power do fifty-year-old women get? They become invisible!" Oh yes, I'm shocking you. I can tell from that forced laugh. You think I'm so bourgeois. A little middle-class cow confusing her own fate with prostitutes and victims. A hysteric. That's your diagnosis, isn't it? Another one who thinks with her uterus. Is that what it says in your file? Or worse? Psychotic? Narcissistic? Paranoid? But *you're* the bourgeois: the one with enlightened views about what's normal, what's abnormal, the difference between whore and hormonal. You don't know anything, Marc, don't go believing you do. What do you know about women, Marc?

Sometimes I so wish I were a man. It would be restful.

Here? You're right, let's change the subject, let's keep it courteous.

No. Here I'm seen. Everyone sees me here. So I'm staying. In Africa, I can't remember which country it's in, Rwanda, I think, when they say hello, they say "I see you." Isn't that wonderful! We count our likes on Facebook, we count the thumbs-ups on our profile photos, but the meaning's the same. The thing is we don't just want to be seen, we want to be seen in a good light. So we make ourselves younger, prettier, we big ourselves up. We resist erosion. We don't want to melt into the crowd, we don't want to get lost. I think that's perfectly understandable.

But in my case there was only one I wanted. I wasn't interested in being seen, or even seen in a good light. I wanted to be *recognized*. For someone to say: there she is! You know, like when a baby's born, when the father recognizes the child.

Ah, okay, now the analyst is stirring—I thought as much! My father recognized me, yes, of course, don't read too much into it. But he wanted a boy, like everyone in the world. I was the second daughter, the disappointment. When I say I want to be recognized, I mean with all the gratitude of recognition, re-cognition: it's her, and I'm happy it is. There she is, here I am, and the link between us can't be denied, can't be erased. Indisputable. Inalienable. "I recognize you and I recognize how precious your existence is."

I did the exact opposite, it's true. Such cruelty, Marc. You won't let me get away with anything. But it's true. I sent a picture of someone else, so I had no chance of being recognized, you're right. Fine, okay, it's the other way around, the opposite is true: maybe I wanted to die, deep down. A woman's always threatened with death. Never safe, ever.

Deep inside her, there's this insecurity, this dependence: being female. Wanting to see what it was like, then, being forced to die. Being able to live only as a ghost. Haunting the Web as if hiding behind a veil. That's what I was saying earlier—a death wish, is that what you call it?—a death wish can be for yourself or for someone else. It's hard to unravel.

On the other hand I've never felt so alive as I did in the few months of that virtual relationship with him. I wasn't pretending to be twenty-four, I *was* twenty-four. A vestige of my time as an actress, maybe. And of memories. And desire. I slipped into character with all the ease of an actor. There was no established script so I improvised from what my partner offered me, I parried his shots. Every time Chris and I talked on Facebook, I heard the part I had to play in his words, I sight-read my score as a mirror of his, I became his ideal, his alter ego, his dream woman, the one men dream up with their eyes open. I played opposite him, literally. But it wasn't an easy part, my whole being was gradually molded, reconfiguring itself out of love—yes, I think that's the right word, love, doesn't that mean surrendering yourself to someone, falling into them, no longer belonging to yourself?

And anyway, the character wasn't that far removed from me, you know. For instance, Claire Antunes really wasn't that computer literate—like me. She was more than twenty years younger than me—a generation (I could have been her mother, oh my Lord)—but we had a lot in common: the shyness, the dreams, the search for love combined with a real longing for freedom, or at least autonomy (she earned a living, wasn't dependent on a man or her parents), a liking for the arts (photography). Despite her age, then, there was nothing geeky about her. So I didn't have to strain my abilities to play the fool when Chris suggested we Skype: "What's Skype?" He never brought it up again. He liked me like that, a bit out of it, a bit spacey. Sentimental. A pure little soul waiting for love. He didn't fit in either, in his own way. I had a sense of that. But didn't know it yet.

It stayed friendly for a long time, yes. He went off to Goa in March, late March I think, he messaged me from over there saying he wanted to get to know me better, we'd been live-chatting for three months. With him so far away it was easier for me, I felt freer to talk to him because there was no danger of it leading to a meeting. Mind you, he invited me to go see him over there—he and Joe had just rented an apartment near the beach. "Would your friend not mind if I turned up?" I asked. "No, he's totally cool, and anyway he has people over too." That last bit hurt me a lot less than I was afraid it would—at least, if it hurt me it was less in relation to Joe than because I found myself lumped into a generalization: people. I didn't know whether Chris was having the same conversation with his girlfriend or other girls on Facebook, I might have thought so if I'd believed what Joe had told me about him. But I didn't think he was. In fact, I was convinced I was the only one having such a peaceful yet passionate relationship with him. I could tell he was snared, bitten—no, I don't like such obviously animal metaphors that imply a hunter and prey—not bitten, then, but smitten, and I was too. I already seemed unique to him, already stood out from the crowd, from people. Love means electing, not selecting. We'd mutually elected each other.

Our Internet conversations had gotten more intimate with the distance, he talked about his plans, involved me in them, "you'll see," "I'll show you," I told him I loved his photos, especially the ones of destitute but smiling women that he posted on his wall, he went one further, stressing how dignified they were and how much he admired them, "they're magnificent." Our messages now ended with little hearts and stars, with thinking-of-yous and kisses. Incidentally, I loathed all that, sending or receiving little x-kisses, that's for kids, I send my kids x-kisses. I wished Chris could have found a more mature way of sending kisses, something with a sexual dimension. Those x's are stupid, emasculating, defeminizing, the very neutrality of an x is sexless, don't you think? But I didn't say anything because...

Excuse me? Did I say that earlier? Yes, I remember. I'm not above the odd contradiction, you know. I am crazy, after all. I'm the child, okay? But that's exactly why I was looking for a man who would recognize the woman in the child. Or the child in the woman? Aargh! You're confusing me. Basically, we started exchanging sweet nothings—sweet but they really meant nothing. The things you say when you're not looking someone in the eye. One time I even risked an "I miss you" and "When are you coming back?" He replied "Me too" and "I can't wait." Every now and then, in one of the pictures he posted, I'd see Joe in the background, leaning against a surfboard, chatting with girls, striding naked into the ocean, his jeering expression hardly bothered me anymore, and neither did his tanned body. I studied those images trying to make out the sort of life they had, and my pain was now focused on the absentee, the one holding the camera, any niggle of uncertainty came from what was out of shot. Chris was sort of the likable face of Joe, if you like, the loving side of him, the side I'd missed. He sent me pictures of lotus flowers and marigolds that he'd taken for me. "Little flower," he wrote. The childish sweetness of his words and the hearts he sent gave me something I'd never had, or so little and so long ago: a youthfulness, the tenderness of a first love shared. At the same time I was teaching in college, I was explaining Shakespeare, Racine, Mlle de Scudéry, "love is an unknown quantity that comes from an unknown source and ends in an unknown way." Ah! How it ends, you're telling me I know how it ends! I know it all now. But back then, sitting at my screen, I experienced the relationship without irony, without detachment, without knowing: "I loved, my Lord, I loved, and wanted to be loved." I had become a dual personality, yes, there were two of me, the sweet young blossom and the flower of the university staff. I gave myself free rein.

Ah yes, your predecessor came up with that argument too. It probably worked well for him with his students. I can't tell you how many of my male colleagues married one of their doctoral students! It's become the norm. But it's not the same for a woman. The social recognition and respect generated by professional success or personal charisma are all very well, they're gratifying, but they're not conducive to love. Being respected for your lectures or your books is like a parody of the desire you no longer inspire. Admiration is just another way of killing us, it feels too much like murder, cutting us in two once and for all, the body to one side, the mind to the other, with an ax. "I'm being dismembered here!" we want to scream—but what's happened to our voices? We don't know, we've been brought up not to cry out. Here at least I can scream. *Aaaaah!*

It feels good. Yes and no. No one can hear it.

You can, yes. But you're being paid to. You're paid so that everyone really gets the fact that it's not love, you and me.

So, to be honest, it wasn't worth it.

See you tomorrow.

Me? Yes, I knew what Chris looked like. First of all there was his profile photo, and anyway he was never shy about posting pictures, he was even quite proud of the way he looked, and so he could be—insofar as we have any right to be proud of something beyond our control. I'll show you some pictures if you like. You won't find them on Facebook, both our profiles were taken down a long time ago, and with good reason! But I printed out several, I still have them. I also saw him in a video that Joe showed me. A handsome guy, really. Tall, slim, nicely put together. Like Joe. With three days' worth of stubble, mountaineer style, very sexy. A bit of a cliché, I know. But I like all those outward signs of virility, I don't go in for subtlety, I lap up the Latin lover look. Chris played on that a lot, he made quite a point about his height, for example—six feet one inch. One time he asked me how tall I was, I lied, I made myself shorter, he sent me a picture of himself next to a foldout measuring stick, and he was pointing to where I would come up to on him, just about under his shoulder. It was almost annoying, puerile anyway, the way he promoted his physical assets—except maybe it actually showed great perceptiveness?

It reminds me of that terrible passage in *Belle du Seigneur*. Have you read it? You're not very cultured, Marc. How can you claim to plumb the human heart without reading all the great connoisseurs of the human heart? It's absurd. Basically, Albert Cohen created this emblematic male character, Solal, who compares men's rivalries regarding women with the physical battles between baboons: male baboons fight over females and the strongest wins, and the strongest is the tallest, and the one with the best teeth. If he's ten centimeters shorter or has a front tooth missing, then no more lust for him and no more great love stories! Cohen makes us look like idiots, us women, but aren't men worse, infinitely more dependent on our beauty, our appearance?

It's enough to make you cry, if you stop to think about it.

In the end I was like all the rest, I'm just like everyone else, his looks kindled my desire. It works both ways, the absolute prestige of beauty. Personally I've never understood the supposed difference between women's beauty and men's. How many times have I heard that cliché: "A woman is much more beautiful than a man!" And both sexes agree on that, it's a triumph of popular opinion. Well, I don't think so. Aesthetically speaking, breasts are no more fascinating than a muscular torso. I take as much pleasure looking at a handsome man in the Métro or at a jogger's legs as I do admiring a top model on the cover of a magazine. At least, I did.

Oh! It's not worth it: they come to me. And if you want proof, you're here yourself. No, no, don't bother protesting, Marc, I'm being serious, you're good-looking, you're very good-looking. And there are some young guys here who play basketball, they're in rehab, failed suicides, you must have seen them. That's enough for my contemplation. And my pain. Beauty makes you suffer if no one thinks to offer it to you.

The phone came before the photo, yes. Chris gave me his number right away, but I didn't call him for several months. The first time must have been in mid-May, he'd just come back from Goa and had headed straight to Lacanau, apparently to show off the videos he'd made and to work on his photo-reportage—I think none of it ever actually saw the light of day. I hid my number and called him one evening, late, on an impulse, in distress, I was home alone, it was my week without my kids, I needed something real. He picked up, I could hear a radio or a TV in the background but he went somewhere private straightaway, he said "Hello," the mental picture of Joe slumped on a sofa vanished almost before it appeared. I said, "Chris, it's me, it's Claire, talk to me." He was immediately focused, that's what was wonderful, the instinct between us, I could hear in his voice that he was aware how fragile that moment was, he didn't have my number, I had his, I could vanish and he wanted me to stay, he wanted to keep me. I heard all that in his voice, which was instantly tender, gentle, very gentle, as if he were speaking to a little girl. His voice protected me, gave me shelter, reassured me, his voice prioritized me—nothing like that acerbic "Go die." He started talking about himself, his time in Goa, the people he met there, his work, how he wanted to become a well-known photographer. He said—not for the first time—that his art was his life, he told me he liked Guns N'Roses and Nirvana, but also rap and reggae, dance music, "I'm sure you like dancing," he said to get the conversation started and I said yes and it's true, I've always loved dancing, even here we have parties, will you come to one, Marc? Do you dance, Marc? If I don't take my medication I dance really well, you'll see. I laughed and said I'd had too much to drink and I had, I'd been drinking to resist the urge to call him, to make him a carnal reality, the human voice is carnal, it tells you something about a person's body, don't you think? And then I'd gone on drinking to be sure I succumbed to the urge to call him, and I'd done it, but I was shaking so much that I came across more drunk than I was, and I was very careful about what I said, I was frightened I'd give myself away, that my voice would betray me. "I love your voice," he murmured. "But how old are you exactly?" I mumbled, my heartbeat accelerated, what if I'd ruined everything by calling him? I suddenly panicked, I wasn't even sure what birthdate I'd put on Facebook. Luckily he said, "Twenty-four, is that right?" I said, "Yes, nearly twenty-five," and he laughed at my exactness, "You seem younger, I mean, even younger," he said. "You're voice is like a teenager's, I hope you're legal," then he corrected himself, afraid his joke was a bit risky, too sexual, "but with a wonderful tone, I'm crazy about your voice already." He was wrong, of course, you could argue that he didn't have a shred of intuition, that he was making a silk purse out of a sow's ear, but I didn't see it like that at all: he was getting me exactly as I was, in an adolescent state of love. And I was in that state because he wanted me like that, it's that simple. Lacan has something very interesting to say about this, your predecessor had me read an article, I kept it, I'll have to dig it out. Basically, it says love is always reciprocal. Not in the sense that you're always loved if you love — oh my, that would be too perfect — but to the extent that when I love someone, it's not random, that person is implicated in my love, he's integral to it, a prerequisite for it, even, he's the one I love and no one else, and it's quite something to inspire someone's love, it creates a connection, it's not neutral. I like the notion that we can be responsible for the love we elicit, which means that in a way, by failing to respond to it, we respond. With Chris, the two tendencies were almost compounded, for him and for me. So when I eventually sent him the photo of Ka—, um, of the pretty brunette, it didn't feel like a con to me, well, not really, because he already loved me: he loved my voice, he loved my words, the way I thought, and laughed, he told me he did, kept telling me. And you said so yourself: I'm beautiful too. Okay so I'm blond, and older, but nice. So what, then, what was wrong with that? At one point I did wonder whether he was looking for a woman to have children with, that was my one misgiving: if he had dreams of being a father, if that was what he wanted deep down — he was already thirty-six, after all. So I tested him a little, I said he took lots of photos of children, he said, "Yes, kids are beautiful," but I felt he was saying that to please me, because he thought I loved children, and was thinking about them. That was when I told him I couldn't have any, I wasn't lying, even if I did give a false reason, some story about a genetic thing, I don't really remember, either way, he was comforting, he wrote saying a woman could easily be happy without children, "and anyway, if you want them, you could always adopt." He even added, "I'll take you to India," with a winking smiley. "Did you see how beautiful and cheerful they are there, despite the poverty?"

But I've already told you this! I sent a picture chosen at random on Google—a pretty brunette leaning on her balcony on a sunny day, with a V-necked T-shirt and peachy breasts, but decent. What do you mean you don't believe me? Why would I lie? Is it because I couldn't find it to show to your predecessor? I've looked but it was more than two, three years ago, she's gone, I'm guessing turnover is quick on Google, especially with the tens of thousands of images that are thrown out every day. But it really doesn't matter.

Your intuition? Oh, well, now we're in great shape! Listen, I'm tired. Isn't that enough for today?

Hello. You look fantastic. Blue suits you. I'll take the liberty of telling you that, we can say whatever we like in this place, it doesn't commit us to anything. Are you letting your beard grow? Right, what are we talking about today?

Wow, you're tenacious. You're stubborn. I already said it isn't at all important—a photo of a pretty brunette chosen at random. A fake just like so many others on social networks. It was just bait, a lure.

Okay so it is important, because Chris homed in on her, got lost in that image, lost in the illusion. It was wrong of me, okay. Do I have to recite the confiteor or something? Do you think I haven't cried enough? I haven't repented enough?

If you really want to know I think it's disgusting how much a woman has to do to be appealing, to be attractive.

Of course I do it, I do it grudgingly, I've always done it, even when I was very young, I was never the last to buy stupidly expensive face creams and dresses way beyond my budget, with low necklines and everything, like my mother, paying for waxing sessions at the beauty salon, which was agony, at fifteen I bought anticellulite gel with my first babysitting money, I remember putting it on my calves because my boyfriend thought they were too big. No, to be totally accurate, what I really can't stand, what makes me bitter, is the fact that all that fussing about appearance works, it's the only thing that works. I remember if I noticed a man eyeing up my figure in a closely tailored jacket or checking out my ass before coming over to talk to me, I was pleased but also terribly sad. I wished I could be loved for being me, do you see? Without the gym or the clothes or the lipstick. For him to meet *me* and not the artificially created object he was looking for. I remember a coworker who asked me out for lunch one time, he was fat and ugly, we talked about the faculty, about teaching, and in the middle of the conversation he looked at me and said reprovingly, "Why don't you wear lipstick?" Not having to sell myself, to flaunt myself like something on a market stall. A market that sells women, the woman market. Constantly reiterating my sexuality. Being sexy, being...

Aren't you supposed to listen to me rather than interrupt? And why didn't you pick up on "like my mother" instead? Why don't you want to take that idea farther? Let's take my mother farther, shall we? Do my word games not do it for you? Are they baking your brawls? Oh, anyway, damn it, since you're so adamant about this, I'll tell you where I found the photo, I don't give a damn really. It was a picture of my niece, Katia. There, happy now? A lot of good that'll do you...

She was a pretty brunette and Chris seemed to prefer brunettes, that's why! You're a pain, you know.

I put it in the past tense because...because it's in the past, that's all. What would you like me to say, for goodness' sake? What does it matter to you where she is now? What does that have to do with this? Are you fantasizing about her too? No, no, she never knew. Yes, I'm sure of that. Absolutely sure, yes.

Because she's dead. Katia's dead. What difference does that make? She was already dead when I used her photo. I didn't kill her if that's what you're thinking. Do you want me to confess to all the crime in the world? And now I'm out of here, it's time for the writing workshop. See you!

I don't know. Perhaps just because I wanted her to keep on living. One thing really upset me when Katia died, I ended up with her computer among all her stuff, but because neither I nor anyone else knew her password I never managed to get into her Facebook account or, obviously, to shut it down. So her profile's still there, years after she died; if you type in her name (but I won't tell you her name and she used a pseudonym anyway), she turns up, her profile photo with sunglasses (no, another one), her cover picture with a word written in fluorescent yellow: ELSEWHERE. And if you're friends with her, which I was, you can read her last post—her bugle call at the end of the day—some insignificant comment made two weeks before she died, and messages on her wall from her few friends—or coworkers, rather—regretting her passing, kind of paying her their posthumous condolences, sharing the grief or maybe just the news with her, the news of her death. I wonder what profiles like hers are called in Facebook jargon. Not fakes, no. More like ghosts. That's what she's become. A doubly virtual woman—dead but still in limbo on the Internet. So yes, I must have wanted her to keep going somewhere else, yes, ELSEWHERE, for her to be loved, and she was actually loved very little—by a man, I mean—I wanted her beauty to touch someone's heart. We look alike, we looked alike, a little: she's my niece, my brother's daughter. She lived through me, if you like, thanks to that photo. And Chris loved her through me. What's wrong with that?

She committed suicide.

I don't know. We never knew. She was twenty-eight. Her father—my brother—died three years earlier from his injuries in a car crash. His wife was killed instantly, along with my older sister who was with them. He spent three weeks in the hospital, we even thought he'd pull through, he came out of his coma, but then...I had a chance to promise I'd look after his daughter. Katia was twenty-five at the time, no longer a little girl, but she was fragile, she was susceptible to depression, to drinking too much, to letting people manipulate her, and as she was very pretty...Losing her parents didn't exactly help, of course. Soon afterward she lost her job—she was an accountant, I think she was bored out of her mind—and to keep the promise I made my brother, I suggested she come stay with us for a while, so she could get in better shape. I still lived near Rouen with my family at the time. I took the last photos of her in the garden, including the one that I later sent to Chris.

I didn't know her very well, really. My brother lived abroad for a long time, we hardly ever saw them. I grew close to her after her parents died, but she was always a little reserved, at least with me... She behaved like the only child she was, self-sufficient, kind of solitary actually. She didn't tell me much about her friends, she never invited anyone to the house, just being discreet maybe, but she can't have had many anyway because she was new to the area, to the village where we lived. She spent her time on the Internet, it was the early days of Facebook, I remember, but at the time I thought it was dumb, I didn't really know how it worked. Katia would spend hours at her computer, which irritated me because she was setting a bad example for my kids, they were young and easily influenced—I wanted to keep them away from all those video games and other garbage. And the rest of the time she tanned herself in the garden, and played Ping-Pong with my husband, or she went to rehearsals for his shows, he gave her minor walk-on roles to cheer her up, that's what he said, they got along well, he said she needed a new father figure.

She left... she left because she had to go sometime, didn't she, she wasn't going to stay with us *ad vitam aeternam*, was she? I found her a little job as an accountant's assistant in a cleaning company near Rodez. How? By scouring the work pages of the local paper myself, seeing as she wasn't doing it. "Seek and ye shall find: it's true of work as well as husbands," my grandmother used to say. She didn't really want to leave, obviously, she was happy with us. But I thought my brother and sister-in-law wouldn't like her to be idle, at her age. I thought I was doing the right thing. But I got it wrong. I helped her move to Rodez. She took up her job, she wasn't earning much but it seemed to be working okay. Even if she never got in touch herself to tell us her news, whenever I called her, she seemed to be doing okay. I couldn't have guessed, you see. We never found out what happened. The police didn't investigate because they quickly concluded that it was suicide. Not murder or an accident. Suicide.

Why? First of all the studio door was locked from the inside. There were no signs of a struggle. No note to say goodbye either, mind you. A bottle of gin with quite a dent in it. But most significantly her wrists weren't broken, that was established at the autopsy. Apparently if you're pushed or you fall accidentally, you instinctively put your hands out, even if there's no point, even from the fifth floor, and you break your wrists. But if you throw yourself out voluntarily...

It reminds me of the story about the guy who fell from the twenty-fifth floor. At each floor he thinks, "Everything's fine so far..." Do you know that one? Wait, I have a better one. It's a woman who's falling from the twenty-fifth floor. She's caught on the twentieth floor by a man on his balcony and he asks, "Do you fuck?" She says no and he drops her. On the fifteenth floor she's caught by a man who asks, "Do you suck?" "No," she stammers. He lets go of her. She continues to fall but on the tenth floor she's stopped by a man and she frantically stutters, "I'll fuck and I'll suck." "Whore!" says the guy and throws her on down.

Okay. You don't find that funny. I love jokes, especially dirty ones. You're a puritan. Shame. What I mean is, she didn't find the right man, who would accept her as she was.

When I was allowed into Katia's place, they'd done their searches and hadn't found anything, no clues, no suspect connections. The people where she worked said she was nice, not very sociable; no one had ever known her to be in a relationship despite how beautiful she was. They described her as the dreamy type, often gazing out the window.

There wasn't much in her studio, a few folders with administrative papers, bills—I sorted through everything in search of the tiniest detail to shed some light on her private life in the three months she'd spent in Rodez. Nothing. I'd been given her cell phone: nothing—numbers for her coworkers, for a hairdresser, the bank, our numbers. And her parents', which she hadn't deleted. There was just one unknown number, and I called it to see: it was unavailable. I thought her computer would have more to say, but her emails didn't tell me anything, not one was compromising, or even private, maybe she'd deleted them before deleting herself. Her life—twenty-eight years of life—seemed empty, smooth, with not a hitch except her parents' deaths, she'd kept all the newspaper clippings. The only thing that intrigued me were the ads on her computer, the cookies, you know what I mean, the ones that follow you and keep tabs on you the whole time. There were ads for dating sites, Meetic, eDarling, that kind of thing. She must have had an account, and I did everything I could to find it, but without the password what could I achieve? I even asked the police to run a computer inquiry to decode Katia's digital secrets. They didn't want to. They felt there was nothing to justify such an intrusion into her private life—the dead are entitled to respect too, they told me. But what if some creepy guy on Meetic or something like it drove her to this, I screamed, isn't that a crime?

Is that not a crime?

Is that *not* a crime?

But no. Nothing illegal in that. Or you'd have to prove moral harassment, find evidence of intent to cause harm. And then some...What about me, then, did I have any intent to cause harm? The police also told me that with suicides, it isn't always premeditated, and there isn't necessarily a specific reason. Hence the absence of clear warning signs, or a suicide note. Katia could have opened the window for a bit of fresh air, because she was hot, and could have propelled herself over the railings on an impulse, a sort of *raptus*, before anyone has time to see, I'm gone. As if bringing an end to a problem, a terror, a colorless existence, or just an attack of the blues, that's all. But I don't believe that. I think she'd met someone on a dating site or on Facebook, who knows which? and she landed herself a nutcase, a cruel guy who made her suffer so much it killed her. A "go die," in other words! So she's dead. That's what she died of. People don't die, they're killed. I kill, I am killed. It's the natural trajectory of life, to kill and be killed. No one gets away.

Right, bye. There goes the bell.

I've brought you some evidence of what I was saying the day before yesterday. It's the book Katia was reading when she died. I've left the bookmark where I found it, on page 157. She'd almost finished it, and she'd turned some pages over, you'll see, they're significant. I was shocked when I saw it on her bedside table. All her books were neatly lined up on shelves, nothing very exciting, I looked at them one by one—some *Famous Fives* that she'd kept since childhood, accounting manuals, a few detective stories, a treatise on happiness. On happiness! And then this book. I can tell you, I went through it with a fine-tooth comb, read it and reread it. And not just because it was the last depository of my niece's life, in a manner of speaking. I also read it simply because I was interested in it. I'd just met Joe. Here, listen to this, she highlighted it in yellow:

Much as this contradicts common preconceptions, the hysterical man (HM) does not like making love. In the worst 57 *cases, sex can even be a chore to him and affords him very little pleasure. What HM is interested in is the process of seduction, of arousing expectations and then systematically disappointing them. At this point he dumps you unceremoniously and starts fantasizing about his next prey, the next dupe. The typical HM: Don Juan, condemned to wandering from one woman's needs to the next, but frustrating them all. His motto: The grass is always greener somewhere else. The modern-day HM is increasingly widespread and spends his life online: on porn sites, dating sites, or gaming, they all shield him from making real-life connections. He is infinitely happier masturbating or meeting up with his buddies. If you commit the folly of marrying him, he will very quickly turn you into a fishing widow, golf widow, or the like. HMs make women suffer but we should not forget that they suffer too. Indeed, unlike narcissists, they feel guilty because they are unable to stop themselves from sabotaging any situation that appears smooth and harmonious,*

and from making potentially successful relationships fail.
They always look for the flaw in a woman, and they find
it: with one fatal sentence they get through the crack in
your armor, and leave you there. To be avoided at all costs
if you are looking for love: an HM will never have the same
agenda. Unless you yourself are a hysteric, in which case
the relationship will function on the principle of reciprocal
frustration! Food for thought!

Yes, I know, I know, I can see you wincing, okay, so it's
not Freud! Mind you, reading this makes me think Katia
must have been hiding a lot. She earmarked lots of other
pages, you'd think she'd met every lunatic on earth. There
was probably a parallel dimension to her social life, full of
fantasies, neuroses, and dubious acquaintances. My brother
was pretty strict, she had a sheltered upbringing, she with-
drew from the world. You can see that in the photo: she's
smiling but in a restrained sort of way, she's holding back
her smile. The problem with playing hide-and-seek is when
you stay hidden and nobody notices. If everyone stops
playing when you're still tucked away behind a bush, what
happens to you? Losing the game isn't about being found;
losing it is when no one's looking for you. The only solution
left is to open a window and fling yourself out of this life.
Yes, neuroses. That word brings you up short, doesn't it?
Let's say I tried to piece together what might have happened to her. And I wanted to give her a second chance,
in a way. A second life. But that was after the fact. First
I fell in love with Chris, then I sent the picture of Katia.
Not the other way around. That's significant. And if there's

one person who didn't seem to be a tricky personality, it was Chris. I already told you "cool" was his catchphrase. He adapted to me so easily it was touching. So I loved children? Well, he wanted three. I couldn't have any? He didn't mind at all. I longed to travel? He had wanderlust in his soul. I dreamed of a little love nest? He wanted to settle down. I hated jealous men? He wasn't the jealous type. I was looking for a close, almost symbiotic relationship? So was he. He wanted to be my Prince Charming. I was moved by his eagerness to please me, to accept me, till then I'd experienced pretty much the opposite, I'd always complied with my partner's wishes and tastes, so I suddenly thought: this is what love is. It's someone who agrees to share me with me.

Guilty, yes, of course, because I couldn't do anything, plus I'm the one who drove her out of the house. Well, I mean, not drove. I just needed to be alone with my family again, especially as things weren't that good with my husband, I wanted to focus on us again. That failed in a big way: we separated three months later, and Katia's dead. And then there was Joe. And Chris. And I went crazy.

Crazy? What I mean by crazy? Are you asking me? Are *you* the one asking *me*?

It means seeing the world as it is.

Smoking life without a filter. Poisoning yourself right at the source.

Katia must have seen with that sort of clarity. At some point, she saw the absence of love, so she absented herself.

It's different for me. What I saw was loss. Not someone absent. Someone lost. Like lost time. The time I spend with you, for example, that's lost, it's wasted. I get the feeling you want to make me say something, but only you know what!

My husband came this morning with the kids, yes, your information is correct, news travels fast. I couldn't see them, I was afraid he'd be with his new wife—and their visits upset me, it's all over, all that business, I'm no longer part of that world. Let's talk about Chris instead if you're keen to keep talking. I've been dreaming about him and in the writing workshop this afternoon I wrote a page of beautiful text about him, well, I thought it was. Camille seemed pleased.

After that first phone call, there were others. It was very sweet and very ordinary, but every time we ended a call I had this love anxiety—a fear of loss that I always experience alongside love. I tried reasoning with myself, saying, "This whole thing's a fabrication. He's in love with you, but it's not you. You're in love with him, but you don't know him." But I also kept thinking of Antonioni's wonderful words from I'm not sure which film: "Love is living in someone else's imagination." A fabrication, yes. So what? Being loved means becoming the heroine. Love is a novel that someone else writes about you. And the other way around. It has to be reciprocal, otherwise it's hell. So the two of us loved each other, Chris and I really loved each other: I lived in his imagination, there's no doubt about that, and I could tell I was alive inside his head. And I couldn't stop thinking about him. I tried to picture his life from the information he gave me. An adolescent phrase such as "I went to the dentist with my mother" or "My grandfather is in the hospital" precipitated me into a state of delirious, loved-up empathy. He talked earnestly about being short of money, his artistic ambitions, and how the one was thwarting the other. And everything he said was laced with very gentle, slightly naive words which left me defenseless: "You're my ray of sunlight," "Don't forget me," "I want to talk about you to everyone all the time." But he still called what we had friendship, and so did I. I wondered what Joe—assuming Chris was confiding in him—what Joe thought of such a platonic relationship. He must have thought it completely ridiculous!

Our conversations almost always happened late in the evening. I often talked quietly so as not to wake my kids during the weeks when I had them, and Chris even ended up asking me why. I hung up quickly without answering, but that triggered a whole new raft of lies. The lies became even more essential when he left Lacanau in June because Joe's family was taking over the house for the whole summer. Chris didn't move to Paris where he couldn't afford the rent, he explained one evening in a very soft, controlled voice, so he went to his parents' in Sevran. Not very glorious, he said, at nearly thirty-seven, to be back in the suburbs with Mommy and Daddy but he had no choice. How about you, he asked, are you happy where you're living? You're in Pantin, is that right? That's real close to Paris. I hope I'll come see you soon.

I felt more and more cornered by this dangerous proximity, I couldn't keep this up indefinitely, finding excuses not to meet, so I invented a new snag. I "admitted" to him that I sometimes spoke very quietly because I lived with someone, with a... well, I didn't live alone. At first he thought I meant a roommate, but I told him it was my boyfriend. He took the hit, his voice sounded thicker which constricted my heart. "For a long time?" he asked. "No," I told him. "And things are already not good between us. He's very jealous, very suspicious." Chris agreed with me wholeheartedly, emphatically: he couldn't stand jealousy either, it was a despicable emotion, and truly loving relationships should be based on trust. "I'm not like that at all," he said. "And do you have anyone?" I asked. "No, I'm single," he replied with a vehemence tinged with reproach. I'd guessed as much: someone called Audrey, twenty years old with one child, a supermarket checkout girl in Bordeaux, had recently disappeared from his list of friends. He'd broken up with her. He was all mine.

I know, it was the perfect opportunity to end this impossible affair. But I didn't want to. I couldn't. Every time I took a step toward breaking up with him, I'd take one step back to win him over again. I needed to hear his voice, to know what he was doing. I needed to feel loved by him. He'd replaced Joe, and if I lost him I'd be alone. He was proof that I existed. You know, the sad thing is, well, the sadly banal thing, tragically banal, is that this fake admission of a rival actually strengthened the connection between us. Chris thought he was jealousy-free but he was riddled with it. With the sort of jealousy some would call homosexual, no, infantile, Oedipal, would you say?—Can you shed any light on that?—either way, it was as if introducing another man into the frame sharpened his desire, his urge to conquer. Jealousy is three-way love, isn't it?

From then on, because they were secretive, clandestine, our conversations took an erotic turn. Sometimes I'd hang up with no warning (my son was having a nightmare) and Chris would send a concerned, almost anxious message on Facebook, a lover's message. He shuddered at the thought that I might stop calling him, or someone could force me to stop, he was consumed with fear of losing me, but I realized this only afterward. I reveled in these conversations made all the more intimate by the secrecy surrounding them, I looked forward to them, longed for them. Of course sometimes doubts would creep in, feelings of disappointment. I was used to more intellectual connections with men, I was one of those people who wonder how anyone can live without reading Proust. Just talking about the weather rather than whether life was worth living, about TV series rather than the sheer power of desire, all surface and no depth—that was new for me. Well, it was the same with Joe, but his physical presence changed everything, sensuality dispensed with words, people never miss Proust when they're making love. So sometimes I'd hang up and promise myself I'd never call him again because he would never have a body. But I wanted him more and more fiercely, his voice and the image I had of him had me in their clutches. I dreamed of stroking the parts of his body I could see in his photos: his neck, his shoulders, his mouth. Then the conversation would start up again on Facebook.

One evening he asked me for my phone number, I resisted, saying my partner—whom I'd baptized Gilles— couldn't bear him calling, but he insisted, he'd be careful, he'd call when I was traveling, or only when I said he could, but he needed this sign of trust from me, he felt excluded, felt he didn't exist in my life, he needed to have some part of me. I didn't want to give him my number because I was afraid Joe might see it one day, work out that Claire Antunes was me and tell Chris. That was what I dreaded most. So the next day I bought a little phone with a cheap sim-only contract, two euros a month for two hours of calls, unlimited texts, and a number only Chris would know. When I didn't have my children with me I told him he could call, saying either that I was on a business trip or that my boyfriend was away. Chris became a witness to both my "conjugal" problems and my faithfulness: I didn't want to meet him, I explained, because I was afraid I'd fall in love with him and therefore cheat on Gilles. Chris said he understood (he understood everything!), but I should be honest with myself. "I'm convinced that one day our lives will be connected," he wrote. It was a discreet way of saying he loved me, and I liked that discretion, that restraint. He was waiting, he had faith in the future, in us, he wasn't trying to take power. "Let's learn each other," he often said, "there's plenty of time." It felt good, restful, turning to him, not being under any pressure. No pressure from him, I mean. Because *I* was putting myself under pressure. My life revolved more and more around this relationship. I was neglecting my teaching commitments, feeling frustrated with my students, and my children complained that I wasn't really there. I was living for a happy ending that I knew was utterly impossible, I was torn in two, I was going crazy.

Yes, I thought of it, of course I did. It was even a recurring daydream: I'd meet him in a café, in the street, me, the forty-eight-year-old Claire, and he'd fall in love with me—with me and not someone else. Why not, after all?

But to achieve that I needed to be rid of the twenty-four-year-old Claire, or I needed *him* to be rid of her, because I didn't think he could so much as look at another woman while he was in the passionate state we'd reached. For him to love me, for my face to replace Katia's, he had to lose all hope of meeting his perfect young e-pal. So Claire Antunes, my avatar, had to die in order for me to come into his life. And comfort him in his grief. You have no idea how often I pictured the rest of the story, or the *possible* rest! One time I even tried to act out my dream. Chris was coming back from Lacanau, he'd told me what time he would arrive at Montparnasse Station, I'd invented some job out of town, as usual. And on a whim, with no premeditation, at the appointed hour, I put on a pretty dress and went to wait for him on the platform. I hung back slightly, I was planning to follow him but didn't really know what would happen, I needed to see his real body moving somewhere that wasn't just one of my daydreams. I suddenly saw him walking along the platform, carrying a big traveling bag, looking tired and lost, really lost, like a child who's been sent on a journey alone. Then, just as I was hastily improvising what might happen next, a man stepped toward him, a man who looked both gruff and kind, and he took one of the handles of Chris's bag—his father, he would tell me later when Claire Antunes revealed that she'd been there, at the station, that she'd lied when she'd claimed she was out of town. I was touched by seeing him for real, handsome but vulnerable, incredibly vulnerable, I remember thinking that, amazed to see his father waiting for him, at thirty-six years old, just to take him back to the suburbs. And I should have thought

65

about that a bit more, realized how weak he was. But I was blinded by my need for him to be strong, all I wanted to see was the conqueror.

Things could have been so different.

I didn't have time. Chris didn't give me time to orchestrate my arrival on the scene. Besides, he didn't even notice me that day. I made sure I walked past them, him and his father, neither of them saw me, I know they didn't, Chris looked right through me like a window. No hint of intuition in the air, nope. The meeting stayed in the realms of imagination.

But the whole story's written down, you know. In last year's writing workshop here, Camille suggested we work on the theme "Changing the Premise." The idea was to take our own experience as a starting point, a disappointing, unhappy or tragic experience (all of us here have plenty, and spectacular ones at that, you must have lots of grist for your mill), the idea was to imagine a different version, a new development, a possible ending, to invent a narrative that would reorient the actual course of our lives. You can imagine how I threw myself into that project! First of all, I missed writing. I don't mean academic writing and articles for conferences. I've never understood where I get the energy—which I've had for years—to research the most insignificant things and produce reports on them as if the whole world will be transformed or become a better place: the date on a letter from La Rochefoucauld to Madame de Lafayette, the supernumerary comma in a Henry James manuscript, Victor Hugo's propensity for assonance using the syllable -*ance*. The fear that that shows, when you come to think of it! What an escape from real life! No, I mean personal writing, the process of giving outward expression to things imprinted inside us—writing to describe our experiences, our dreams and longings, using a net made up of words to catch them like a writhing fish. Have you ever tried, Marc? Of course it's often disappointing: the contrast between the story inside your head and the one you actually—painfully or otherwise—bring into the world can be terrible. A fish is always more beautiful undulating in the current than gasping in the wind; its scales shine more brightly in the river than in the mesh of a landing net. But while you're tracking it, you're happy. Well, I'm not sure "tracking" is the right word, it's got too much of the hunter about it. It would be better to stick to fishing metaphors. Writing is like fishing—angling, coarse fishing—it's quite physical, but the main thing is the waiting. An active, alert sort of waiting. The feeling that if you wait in the right way, if you know how to wait, listening out for the tiniest quiver of the line, the smallest tremor, you won't be disappointed, it'll bite. Writing is like love: you wait, and then it bites. Or not, as my son would say. Except in love we're often the fish. Aargh, I'm getting tied up in my own fishing line. So anyway, in the workshop I wrote the story as it could have happened if I'd had the nerve. I imagined what could have happened between Chris and me if I'd dared to introduce myself to him—without admitting I was his mysterious Facebook friend, no, I couldn't have gone that far, I'd have been too afraid, too ashamed—just to introduce myself as me, a new acquaintance. I let myself get carried away in my dreams, it was wonderful, oh it was so wonderful.

Obviously, even then I had to choose between several possible endings, happy or otherwise. You'll see. I might give it to you to read one of these days, when I've finished it. My relationship with Chris, in novel form. It's one way of getting the two of us to live together, of animating our ghosts, our virtual bodies, our silent souls, our unspoken words. Camille likes what I've written.

The greatest thing about the workshop is that afterward we're going to play a version of that game they call Exquisite Corpse—sorry for the choice of words, given the circumstances, but that's what it's called, Exquisite Corpse, you really should read more, Marc, this is ridiculous. A surrealist game, then. Except that in this instance, once our stories are finished, what we're going to do is pass it along to the next person so he or she can add a chapter or a page, a different ending. Something we can't see ourselves. Another person's fiction projected onto our own. Each person's dream dreamed by another dreamer. I like the idea, the idea that we don't write everything, that we also get to be written. That things can be seen differently. That things can happen differently.

Why outside? I can't, not outside. I just can't. I've tried. I always came back real soon, I was brought back. My kids are kind. But you can't wait, outside. People live, outside. I don't have anything left to live. I'm not living, I'm waiting for life.

Writing? Yes. Waiting, writing: it's all the same.

But I can't. Don't you understand anything? What sort of relationship could I have with another man? I want *him*.

For fucking, you mean? Don't worry on my account: if anyone wants a fuck it's just as easy here as on the outside. If you want it.

No.

No.

I don't know.

No.

You don't know anything about it.

No.

Leave me alone. I'm tired.

I watched you walking over then, across the grounds, you looked like a cop. Or a crime prevention officer. The way you stopped to talk to people. You looked as if you were running an undercover inquiry. When everyone actually knows you, if you see what I mean. It's like in inner-city ghettos: when you talk to people, they only tell you what they feel like saying. They lie, too. They want peace.

So what's your question, then, inspector?

Ah! Death. Of course, death. That's what you're asking. "That is the question."

Some evenings I could hear so much fear in Chris's voice, at the thought of losing me, so much that I always ended up reassuring him: things were going really badly with Gilles, he was jealous, bad-tempered, I didn't know what to do. "Leave him," he told me. Yes, but where would I go? I didn't have enough money to rent somewhere on my own, I explained. Chris didn't reply, unhappy that he couldn't offer me anything, that his financial situation was even worse than mine. At this point I felt guilty—me in my comfortable two-bedroom apartment on the rue Rambuteau—playing up my "precarious" circumstances on the phone.

But sometimes I was also frustrated by his inertia. He was living with his parents also because he didn't want to look for work. He'd lived off Joe for a while, and now he could have found a job waiting tables or something. But he didn't want to. "I'm devoting myself to my art, I don't want to waste my talent," he'd say between drags on his cigarette—I could hear him exhaling the smoke, it titillated me having that tiny access to his body; maybe he was smoking joints, I asked him one evening, he was indignant, no, he'd stopped all that, he was clean. One time he was dismissive of a photography job I found for him on the Internet. I'd sent him the link on Facebook, it wasn't fantastic, weddings, family ceremonies, but still, it would have gotten him out a bit. But no. He was acting out the part of the impoverished artist for his own benefit: impoverished, forsaken, and noble in his destitution. He wanted to be Depardon or no one. Meanwhile he spent a lot of his time watching American TV series online, so really nothing special. His unwillingness also proved that he wasn't prepared to do absolutely anything for me, to win me over. It's also what convinced me I could break up with him without too many misgivings, you see. Sometimes I got confused, wondered what I was still doing in this mish-mash, this mash-up of several lives. How did I ever think…?

To be honest, I really didn't know what to do anymore. If I came up with a ploy to "dump" him gently—and that would mean dumping myself too, dumping the young woman in me—he talked to me on the phone in such a velvety voice that I lost all my resolve. He described the things we'd do when we were together. He would massage me slowly when I came home tired in the evening, he would cook me pasta carbonara, his specialty, we'd go for drives in his "clapped-out but cool" Citroën DS—she's an old lady, he said, she's forty-five years old. And I blushed privately at my end. He never said anything more explicit, never, for example, made cheeky references, and certainly nothing overtly sexual. I didn't know whether he was afraid of scaring me off or just wasn't that interested in sex. That hypothesis bothered me because, as far as I was concerned, some evenings his voice alone was enough to liquefy me, I'd hang up in the grips of unmentionable longing. Once or twice I commented on how many pretty "chicks" had liked the posts on his wall, he replied reassuringly that this was standard for a photographer, models are always scouting for possible shoots. So I thought maybe he wanted to show me that he didn't see me as a quick fuck but something altogether different. And that was right. One evening he posted a video of Patti Smith singing "Because the Night Belongs to Lovers"—wonderful song, do you know it?—and out of all the possible quotes from it, he chose to make his comment: "Love is an angel disguised as lust." I listened to it and thought, if love's an angel then it's sexless. I felt sad but also reassured: even if there were only words between us, we were still lovers.

He was coming in from Sevran to spend the evening in Paris more and more frequently, and it grew harder and harder for me to justify my refusal to meet him. "We could just have a coffee, couldn't we? A decaf," he joked. "I know your man's not cool but still. With a job like yours you must see a lot of people, don't you, surely some are even photographers, aren't they, so why not me?" When I avoided him he'd say, "It's because you know that the minute we meet, everything will become clear. Clear as Claire can be. I'm absolutely sure we were made for each other, and you know it too, deep down, even if you don't want to admit it."

Clear as Claire can be, oh yes, I thought ironically. Very clear indeed. Clear as spring water. But this was hurting. I put up the best defense I could: "You say that because you like the way I look, you think I'm pretty. But you don't know me. Maybe I'm lying to you."

"But I do know you," he retorted, very sure of himself, very steady. "It's nothing to do with how you look, that shows you don't know me. I don't give a damn about that. What matters is who you are. I like who you are. I'm in love with your soul, I can hear it in your voice, in your words. All the same, though," he added, in response to the silence at my end, "I desperately want to take you in my arms." And that simple phrase, "take you in my arms," made me weak at the knees, it floored me.

I couldn't do it, no. I couldn't do it. But one day I posted a song for him on YouTube, a Catherine Ribeiro song called "De la main gauche"—I was supposed to like good French songwriting, after all. I really wanted him to listen carefully to the lyrics when she says,

So this is my distress
This is the truth that's hurting me
I never had an address
Nothing but a fake ID.

But he...Excuse me? Are you kidding? Fine...If you like. It'll give us something different to think about. I warn you, I don't always sing in tune, especially unaccompanied.

Okay, I'll stop, I'll spare your ears. My attempt to confess failed dismally, he didn't get the message, "just a fake ID" and all that... the only bit he latched on to was the end: "I wanted to say I love you / Love you because it feels real." And he replied, "I do too, Claire, I love you," while adding a gentle dig: "Catherine Ribeiro... did your parents listen to her when you were little?" I'd forgotten she was Portuguese by birth, like my avatar! You see, I wanted to reveal the real me but subconsciously I was still Claire Antunes.

Well anyway, it couldn't go on any longer, I was getting bogged down in my fabrications and suffering in real life. He kept pressing me and I'd run out of reasons to refuse to see him, to have a coffee. I had to break it off, there was no other way out. It broke my heart, but one day when I was feeling strong I messaged him to say it was over, and he never replied. I called him and he didn't pick up, I left a long voicemail message. I told him I was getting married to Gilles, that he'd found a job in Portugal and we were leaving at the end of the month, it was all decided: I had to leave the dream behind. I went on to say how much I'd loved him, how much I still loved him, although I knew that this virtual love could never replace love itself. I asked him to stop trying to contact me, besides, I was going to close down my Facebook account and change my cell phone number so that I couldn't give in to my own longings or to his. I told him I was sure he would soon find true love (sadly, I really did believe that). I ended it with the words "kissing you tenderly," and as I said it I wondered whether he would hear the words "tender lie." I feel doubly guilty, do you see, it's overwhelming. I lured him with a fake persona and then let him founder in my lies.

Yes. He let a couple of days go by, probably thinking that a bit of time would wear me down (and he was right: I was feverishly hoping to hear back from him). Then he sent me one last voicemail, a message that was so like him: calm but passionate, humble but self-assured. He said he was sure we were made for each other, that our destinies were bound by love. But also that he respected my decision, it made him very unhappy but he accepted it. He said he'd walk out of my life if that was what I wanted. He'd stop writing me and stop calling me. *Peace and love*, those were his last words.

It took a superhuman effort not to call him back. I fantasized a scene in which I admitted everything to him and he still loved me, but I didn't believe it, I didn't feel up to it and my self-esteem couldn't take the fatal blow. I studied myself in the mirror and thought: "Impossible." I couldn't rival Katia's beauty. And could he have accepted so many lies? So I held firm in my silence, helped out by a trip I made at that exact time—a conference about Flaubert in Brazil: I went without my laptop or my second cell phone. Those ten days were appalling. It was like a terrible, painful molting process: turning back into Claire Millecam, university lecturer, divorcee, single parent, mother of two. Leaving behind Claire Antunes, the happiness of loving and the joy of being loved, sloughing all that off like an old skin—the beautiful Claire, an old skin, a horrible dilemma!

When I arrived home I couldn't take any more. I threw myself at my phone. No voicemails. I turned on my computer: no messages. I wanted to visit Chris's page. It had disappeared. Completely disappeared. I couldn't find his name anywhere, and every trace of his existence, his likes and posts, had been wiped from my wall. Only his private messages were left in my in-box. He'd been stronger than me, more radical, I thought. And it hurt that he'd had this strength, and that this strength was more powerful than his love. At the same time I was not exactly relieved, no, it was too heavy a weight to bear for that, but I felt I'd handed something on, I'd been freed of the duty to give him up. I no longer had to fight because there was no enemy now, or just a powerless enemy—myself. Still, I couldn't give up straightaway: I called again but the call didn't go through, my number was blocked, I couldn't even leave a message. I also tried to get hold of Joe to have some news, indirectly. But Joe was playing dead. I thought he'd gone back to Goa or somewhere else, maybe farther, maybe with Chris. I waited several weeks before canceling my cell contract, but did it eventually. Then I burned the last bridge by taking down the Claire Antunes Facebook profile. And I went back to my old life as if closing the last page of a novel. Battered, crushed. Old.

No.

Or maybe a little. He was no longer prey to my tricks. My imposture crumbled in the face of the power I attributed to him, a power I've always attributed to all men, often with good reason: the power to bounce back, forget, move on. Whereas a woman wages a constant battle to avoid being a victim, to stay strong, or at least dignified. I won't ask whether you've read *Dangerous Liaisons*, I'm sure you haven't. The Marquise de Merteuil says in a letter to Valmont: "For you, for men, the defeats are merely absences of success. In this very unequal match, our fortune is not losing and your misfortune is not winning." There's always another possible woman for a man. Always one he can go back to, at least one. This certainty is engraved in their very structure, that the beloved woman isn't the only woman. That's what I thought, does that make sense? As I saw it, he'd ended up emerging victorious from the fight that I'd always dominated.

No. I saw a psychiatrist to get some sleeping pills, that's all. Come hell or high water, I carried on living, you know. I hadn't lost, that was quite something in itself. My children thought I was sadder than before, that's all. The joy had gone along with Chris, and that was it. I swamped myself with work, comparing the conjunction *mais* in Ronsard's love poems with "but" in Shakespeare's.

No. I found out a month later, maybe more, maybe less, I've lost track of time. One day, when I was bored, I was looking at my Facebook page—my one, the real one, Claire Millecam's page, where nothing ever happened—and I saw I had a message. It was from Joe. Very friendly. He asked for my news, said he still thought about me. Fancy a coffee? I accepted.

He hadn't changed. Still just as...But I didn't give a damn. I couldn't wait more than five minutes before asking with fake nonchalance whether he was still living in Lacanau with his friend, what was his name again, Christian, Christophe?

"Chris?" he asked brightly. "Well, he's no longer with us, would you believe. Right now he's six feet under, the idiot."

I thought I was going to pass out, all the blood drained from my heart, I heard my own voice coming out muffled as if through cotton wool, saying, "But what happened? Chris is dead? What—"

"Yeah! Fucking stupid, his Citroën went into a tree at ninety miles an hour, not a pretty sight!"

"But—how did it happen—his accident?" I held back my tears as best I could while Joe kept talking in the same jaunty voice.

"Pfff, it wasn't an accident. He drove into that tree on purpose. Committed suicide, the poor guy." "Suicide?"

"He'd been really low for a while, he even cried sometimes. A real wreck. And according to the cops there were no braking marks on the road. All that for some broad who strung him along for months. And not just strung him along, strung him up, strung him out, and hung him out to dry. There are some real bitches out there."

"What? Who?" I was shaking, I couldn't breathe.

"Wha'who, wha'who," Joe mimicked me. "Yeah, some chick he met on Meetic or Facebook, I don't remember, her name was Claire, like you—see? I was right to be wary! And he fell head over heels in love with her, and she just kept dangling the carrot on the end of a stick, and when she dumped him he completely lost it, he didn't know what to do with himself, he trailed around like a tortured soul and in the end he offed himself. For a stupid bitch he'd never even met. Lost the will to live. Love makes people so fucking stupid, and he wasn't that clever in the first place... that's why, in case you hadn't noticed, I steer clear of love myself."

No.

Maybe.

No. Leave me.

2

I know exactly why I'm here before you, my dear coworkers. I have no intention of shirking my responsibilities, I acknowledge and accept whatever sanctions you decide to impose on me. But it is essential, before you judge me, that you fully understand the tenets and outcomes of the affair that brings us here today. Of course you've all read Claire Millecam's file, some of you met her long before I did, and my position as a "newcomer" in the establishment as well as my general lack of experience are probably not unrelated to the mistakes I make. Nevertheless, there's a text I'd like to read to you, a text several pages long, one I'm sure none of you has seen, and one that sheds a different light—at least I believe it does—on the decision that I took in all good faith, independently of the consequences. It is an extract of the novel that Claire wrote here, in the writing workshop, over the course of several weeks—to be more accurate, it consists of large extracts copied from the second part of this novel, in which she imagines what her life with Chris could have been like if, without admitting to her initial imposture, she'd had the courage to try embarking on a love affair with him, a love affair she felt was possible and that she dreamed of having. When I read it, I remembered Lacan's words: "Relationships start in the imagination." She entrusted it to me after our first conversations, so I'm not betraying her—not entirely—by reading it to you, and this reading strikes me as vital if you are to get inside Claire's head and if you are to try, by understanding her, to understand me too.

Claire Millecam

FALSE CONFIDENCES

a novel

The story I want to tell is of a love affair that is always possible
even when it appears impossible to those far removed
from the writing of it — since writing is not concerned
with the possibility or otherwise of the affair.
—Marguerite Duras, *Blue Eyes, Black Hair*

At this stage I couldn't get Chris out of my head, I thought about him all the time. It was unbearable to think nothing would ever happen between us; breaking it off would be like turning my back on life. After all, I was crazy about this man, he loved me, he'd said he did, so why give up? Our destinies were bound together, he kept saying so, he was sure of it. Why not put that to the test? It was like being in a film: it would have been unthinkable to take out the pivotal scenes. He'd messaged me saying he'd soon be returning from Lacanau, living with Joe was getting difficult. (I privately sympathized. How could it not be difficult?)

"Really?" I wrote, "What happened?" In fact, Joe was refusing to let Chris work on the Goa reportage, he'd even destroyed some of the videos and photos taken there; and his family was coming for the summer vacation. Chris had already bought his ticket, he was coming back on a Monday, in three weeks' time, he hoped to meet me at last. The time had come to try my luck. And so I decided to meet him for real, as me, Claire Millecam: we'd soon see what happened to love. To do this, I had to eliminate Claire Antunes, or at least make her disappear from Chris's sight lines if not from his memory. I thought about the best way to free up the space taken by this virtual rival for whom I experienced surges of inexpressible, visceral jealousy, a feeling of powerlessness in the face of her youth and beauty. There's no worse rival than one who doesn't exist. Confronted with her, I felt as the sister of a dead child must feel about her parents: quite sure that in their hearts she will never triumph over this ideal. My niece Katia, who was languishing in a psychiatric hospital after her suicide attempt, was the focus of only part of my aggression. Granted, Chris was in love with an image of her; but that was my fault. And I knew she was so messed up by her last failed relationship that I couldn't project my unforgivable resentment on her.

The best way to get rid of Claire Antunes was still…for her to get rid of herself. So I decided to have her go abroad, and as I'd astutely given her a Portuguese name, she could go set up home…in Lisbon. It wasn't really an impulsive move, she explained to Chris in a firm but affectionate message; it was just that her parents lived there and they'd found her an interesting job, better paid than the slavery of her temporary contract, and as things weren't going very well with Gilles, she was leaving to take stock of things — "I might be back in a few months," she

81

said, then added a final "And even if we never meet, I'll always love you." I wasn't making her close the door for good, sensing that I might well want or need to open it again someday.

Chris replied, saying he was very sad, really unhappy, but he'd wait for me. He could come see me in Lisbon too, after all he had no commitments in Paris, nothing to keep him there; he didn't know Portugal, the light there must be glorious, paradise for a photographer. He'd even worked out a perfect route to take in his old Citroën, using minor roads, his imagination fired by the names of villages along the way — Zambugo, Picoto, so pretty! He hoped I'd invite him to join me — which I didn't, for obvious reasons. This move abroad was also convenient because it meant that, because of the cost, I had to stop our phone conversations. I wanted him to forget my voice so that I could talk to him a few weeks later without running the risk of being unmasked in my other identity. But I wasn't too worried. First of all, you don't hear a voice in the same way on the phone as you do in person. And anyway, to make a connection like that, you'd have to imagine it was possible.

I started engineering our first meeting. It had to be natural, as if chance was taking responsibility for shaping destiny. Accosting him on Facebook or meeting through some intermediary was out of the question. I wanted to play this differently, to be unique. Luckily he'd told me what time he'd be arriving at Montparnasse Station on Monday the twelfth. I would wait for him at the end of the platform — I was sure I'd recognize him even in a crowd, he'd sent me several pictures of himself, and he was tall, with that distinctive hair color, rare on a man, chestnut verging on red, auburn hair. He should be alone. I guessed that to reach Sevran, he'd take the Métro, then the high-speed RER, and it would be there, sitting opposite him in the carriage, that I would talk to him, we would meet. I had three weeks before me in which to prepare, I wanted to be beautiful, with not one gray hair, not one pound overweight, sexy but also reassuring, I wanted to be likable, I wanted to be loved.

So it's now Monday. The Métro isn't crowded, I sit down opposite him. I'm forty-eight but I don't look it, he looks up, sees me. I smile at him, he shifts his legs, smiles at me too, sadly — he must still be thinking about his beautiful "one who got away." I wait for one station, time enough to regain some semblance of calm. He's handsome, with a sort of nobility to his face, his eyes an unusual gray-green color, but there's something tired, almost bitter about him that ages him, and there are quite a few gray hairs in among the russet. I feel pleasantly satisfied about this, first because this means the age difference is almost imperceptible, I'm sure of that; but also because I now have a mission: I'm going to make this man happy. I'm frightened, though, I daren't make a move. But I'm scared he's about to get off so I pretend to look at him searchingly and I say, "Excuse me. I feel like I know you. You're not a friend of Joe's, are you? You're a photographer, right?"

He has all his equipment in an open bag on his knee so I look pretty dumb. But he raises his eyebrows in surprise.

"You mean Joël S?" he asks. "Yes, why? Do you know him?"

"I'm Claire Millecam, his former — well, a former friend."

"Oh yes!" he says guardedly. Joe must have talked about me in strictly sexual terms, and he's embarrassed, hindered by the recollection. Or perhaps it's that my name is a painful reminder of his lost love — I'm suddenly annoyed with myself for giving my own name to my rival, how stupid, what poor judgment! But perhaps the opposite is true, perhaps it's thanks to my name that I too can work my way into his imagination.

"We no longer see each other, Joe and I, we fell out," I explain, then add casually, "But don't you live with him?"

"Not anymore. We fell out very recently, but we did it properly, real angry," he smiles conspiratorially. "Joe falls out with everyone. We could set up a club."

He's silent for a while, looks at me very kindly — the visual equivalent of his first messages — courteous, humorous, and with restrained curiosity. I'm afraid that this very restraint will make him stop right there, so I pick up quickly.

"He sent me some selfies of the two of you, that's how I recognized you, and one time he sent me some of your pictures. I really liked them, actually — landscapes, places you'd seen on your travels. Do you do portraits too?"

"Yes, yes," he laughs. "And not just baobabs and giant pandas. People too."

I say bashfully that I'm just finishing a monograph on Marguerite Duras and my editor will need a portrait for the press.

"He usually sends the photographer he works with. But I could ask him to change…If you'd be interested?"

"Of course I'd be interested. To be honest, I'm looking for work, I'm down to my last cent. That would be real cool." He looks at me more closely, more appreciatively. "And it would be a pleasure too. When would you like to do it?"

I blush, not because of the compliment but the subtext of "do it," it sends a shiver through me as if he's put his hand on my knee. I also feel the hot rush of jealousy at the easy way he strikes up an acquaintance, being so frank with another person, so confidently straightforward. I think of all those women on

Facebook, all the women in the Métro, on the train, all the women in every street.

"Um, I don't know. Do you live in Paris?"

"No, I'm staying in Sevran, with my parents — temporarily, I hope. But I can come over whenever you like in my old Citroën, then we can take some shots in the country, it'll make a change. Unless you'd rather have the perennial author pose sitting at the Café Flore, chin in hand."

I laugh, nod my head.

"So it's a deal, then."

I ask for his phone number, and he takes mine.

"Oh, I have to get off here," he says.

"I'll call you," I say as he gathers his things.

"Cool, glad I met you. Speak soon." And he steps off. I watch him walk along the platform with his bag on his back. As the train sets off again I notice a rose wrapped in cellophane in the metal trash can, tragicomic in this incongruous vase. Is that a bad omen? I don't even consider it. I think he likes me. I catch sight of myself and my blue-gray eyes in the black window. Yes, he likes me.

We very soon moved in together — or rather he immediately came to live at my place. He couldn't afford to pay Paris rents and I had the space, particularly when the kids weren't there. I'd always promised myself that never again would I make the conjugal mistake of sharing a bedroom. I wanted to preserve the virginal, intense feeling I had when we first kissed, just after the photo session. We stood over his camera temple to temple, looking at the portraits he'd taken, and we turned to face each other at the same moment; our lips touched softly, then his tongue probed my mouth, inside my mouth...He left quite soon after that, he had a meeting. Oh, let it happen again, let it be just as powerful, both slower and faster than normal time, like an accelerated slow motion of the pulse of life, an ephemeral sense of eternity, oh, give me back this beginning again! It was in the hopes of recreating that first time every time that I adapted the living room for Chris to use. If he feels free, he'll stay, I thought. Love means staying when you have the option to leave. I put the TV into the dining room for the kids, I bought a sofa bed and a desk so he could work on his photographs, he put a sort of Japanese screen between the two rooms, hung his few clothes in my closet, and our life together began. We actually slept together almost every night, mostly in my bed, occasionally on the sofa, I sometimes went and joined him in the middle of the night, waking him with my caresses, he always responded, I attached a lot of importance to his pleasure because it can be confused with love.

"I can feel your love," he would say when he was close to climaxing in my mouth, and he'd whisper "my love" in my ear before we fell asleep in each other's arms, as every coupling reinforced our growing knowledge of each other. But I would often leave again in the early hours, afraid that my puffy eyes and unmade-up face would remind him of what he seemed to forget. And while I pretended to scoff at women's masquerading, I maintained a carefully affected naturalness, a youthfulness that matched how young I felt inside.

He asked me to call him Chris rather than Christophe, not knowing I'd been calling him Chris for months, that I murmured his name to myself twenty times a day, and to my pillow, like a teenager. He very quickly took to calling me "Ever" — a silly nickname that grew out of "Clever Claire." "Ever, my forever, let's run away forever this weekend," he'd say when we headed to Dieppe in his car to eat mussels and fries, or we'd drive just for the pleasure of it. "You're Ever in my dreams," he'd whisper as he held me to him at night, or, closing his eyes and running his fingers over my face, he'd say, "Ever the mystery," and that would make me shudder. But I swiftly batted away the thought that plagued me in the early days: he called me Ever to avoid saying the name Claire, the other girl's name.

We didn't go out much, or separately, didn't mix with each other's friends, by tacit agreement we kept away from them. He'd sometimes dog-sit for an ex — "she's just a friend, nothing more," he said, laughing at my silence — and I very occasionally saw a coworker or a tennis partner but didn't mention Chris to them. We led what could literally be called a private life. But we didn't deprive each other of anything, and rarely of our own selves. The apartment was laid out in such a way that he could work in his corner and I in mine. I went off to teach, he went out to take photos, we were soon back home together. When the kids were there, he showed them how best to frame a shot, they listened to rock together or watched TV. I don't know whether they really got the fact that we were together, because of the separate bedrooms, but they adored Chris — "He's so cool," they chorused. It's true that his casual approach was fantastic for defusing rows. When we were alone, we'd spend ages just lying listening to music or reading, or we'd embark on complicated recipes in the kitchen only to end up in the local bistro. We got along even when there was silence between us, and there was always laughter at the end of every disagreement.

The question of money came up and was dealt with very early on. He didn't have any, his parents couldn't lend him any, he got his tax credits and took on any little jobs that came his way so long as they were related to photography. I already knew all this, but I listened attentively because this was where it was all being played out, I could tell. Something that continues to be so ordinary for a woman — being financially dependent on another person, often an older man — is still an ordeal for a man. And the age difference didn't help at all. The word "gigolo" hovered nearby, the word "cougar" threatened, they had to be dispelled. So I told him money was a movable thing, that what goes around comes around, I was the one who had it today, he would have it tomorrow, it didn't matter. He liked this line of reasoning, it meant I believed in his talent, that I was just giving him an advance on his future success. And I did some networking to find him work: pictures of monuments, professional portraits. He meanwhile offered to put together photo portfolios for actresses, and I struggled to stifle my jealousy. He never missed an opportunity to compensate for his lack of funds with little kindnesses: a rose, some croissants, a cocktail at a bar. The rest of his earnings paid for his gas, the upkeep of his car, and his photographic materials. The crook of his neck, the place Claire Antunes had so longed to rest her lips, was soft and warm to mine.

Two months passed like this, filled with sweet contentment. We were happy in the way you all dream of being. Then one day the trouble started, and it was my fault, entirely my fault, because I'm crazy. This is how. With my degree-level students I was looking at Tasso's influence on European writers and artists from the sixteenth century onward (teaching, which had sometimes been burdensome to me, was now a pleasure. Everything I did seemed to be immediately balanced by Chris's presence). So we were studying the story of Renaud and Armide as told by Tasso in *Jerusalem Delivered*. During the First Crusade the valiant knight Renaud is imprisoned by a beautiful pagan sorceress, Armide. She intends to kill him along with all his Christian companions, but falls in love with him. To secure his love in return, she makes him drink a magic potion which puts him entirely and lastingly in thrall to her. The knight immediately forgets his sacred mission and languishes in the wonderful life the sorceress offers him. She strips him of his armor and sword, and clothes him in sumptuous robes; she arranges feasts, games, and concerts for him, lavishes him with a thousand caresses and invents a thousand exquisite delights. Their love unfolds over many months, steeped in pleasure and idleness. But Godfrey of Bouillon's crusaders cannot accept their friend's fate and refuse to abandon him to such a contemptible existence. They eventually manage to reach him while Armide is away, and find Renaud lying on a bed decked in fine fabrics, surrounded by rare sweetmeats and carafes of heady wine. They hold a shield up to him so that he can see what he has become, and Renaud, who now only ever sees himself in the magic mirror held up to him by his beautiful captor, is suddenly confronted with his true reflection, a pampered man sprawled among his cushions, dressed as a gallant, and utterly disarmed. His former companions have no trouble persuading him to rejoin them in pursuit of conquests. He rises to his feet, picks up his arms and prepares to leave with them.

It is at this point that the legend and, alas, my own narrative meet. Discovering Renaud's decision, Armide is replete with so much love that she cannot believe her lover — who has been deeply besotted with her for months — could leave her. She thinks that the strength of their passion, constantly reinforced with the tenderest gestures, is now so great that no spell is needed to sustain it. In Lully's opera they even sing an admirable duet, I almost cried when I played it to my students:

> No, I would rather lose my life
> Than extinguish my flame,
> No, nothing can change my heart.
> No, I would rather lose my life,
> Than leave the arms of so charming a lover.

And so, putting her faith in the power of love, Armide throws herself at Renaud's feet, confesses to the spells she has cast on him, and swears she will abandon them. "I love you," she tells him. "I betrayed you, I lied to you. But the only truth is that I love you. Keep me with you. For your love, I will undertake anything, I will even convert to your religion if you ask it of me." Renaud hesitates, gazes lovingly and sadly at the enchantress's beautiful face, but is pained by such betrayal. In the end, the hero's duty is stronger than all other emotion. He tears himself away from Armide's sweet supplications and leaves her forever.

I told this story to my students and couldn't get it out of my mind, I was obsessed with it. One question went around and around inside my head: if I admitted to my previous imposture, would Chris still love me? Would he be shocked to have been manipulated like that? Enough to leave me?

In fact, if I'm to be completely honest, that wasn't really the question that haunted me. The real one, the only erosive question I had, was this: Was Chris still thinking about Claire Antunes? Whenever he looked thoughtful or seemed distant, less attentive, the idea tormented me. Did he still love her? Did he love her more than me, with a purer love, like Renaud's for his sacred mission? With an unconditional love? Wasn't I just a fallback, a consolation for losing her? My jealousy was corrosive.

In order to escape this overriding fear, I decided to put our love to the test. But I had many more doubts than Armide, even if nothing about Chris's behavior justified them for any length of time: he showed every sign of tenderness and desire. I had no objective reason to test the strength of our connection. I don't know why I did it. But I did it. I brought Claire Antunes back to life. I made careful preparations, and could think of nothing else; I wanted to ratify our love. First I took out the phone that I'd hidden in a shoebox at the bottom of my closet. I hadn't terminated the two-euro contract, I'd forgotten to. I charged up the battery and listened, quivering, to the last message Chris had left me months earlier. His sad voice made my heart constrict, but with jealousy — a towering, destructive, deranged jealousy. His past annihilated my present life. So I fine-tuned my strategy. I was well aware that I should abandon the idea, shouldn't be playing with fire, but I couldn't back down now, my fear had completely taken over.

The idea was that Claire Antunes would reappear in the form of a lover's ultimatum: having been unable to forget Chris for all these months of silence and distance, she had broken up with her fiancé and now wanted to meet him at last, meet Chris and live with him, because she loved him, she was no longer in any doubt of that. She didn't know what was happening in his life, but if he still loved her too, he should drop everything now and meet her that very evening at the Café Français. She would be there from nine till ten, and no more. He shouldn't try to call her, he should just come, prove his love by being there. If he didn't show up he would never hear from her again. So this was the abrupt but thrilling message Chris would be receiving from me, in the form of a text from my secret cell phone, that same evening, as we were sitting down on the terrace of our favorite restaurant, just a block from my apartment.

At first I only pictured this test as a "double blind": if Chris went to meet Claire Antunes, of course he wouldn't find her there and he'd lose me or I'd lose him, I wasn't sure which. Unless I forgave him. But if the experiment was going to bring an end to my jealous suspicions, I gradually started contemplating confronting him at the Café Français with the gorgeous young brunette whose photo he'd gazed at for so long: my niece Katia. I'd hardly seen her since her suicide attempt, and obviously always in secret; Chris didn't even know she existed. After a long stay at a clinic in the Southwest, Katia had come to Paris to look for work. She'd been living on the rue Roquette for a month, alone and still depressed. I didn't actually know what had driven her to taking a whole packet of sleeping pills not long after she'd moved to Rodez. A relationship that went wrong, most likely, but she'd never wanted to tell me about it, and I hadn't pressed her. Anyway, plagued by my jealous frenzy, I arranged to meet her at the Café Français at nine that evening. In my nightmarish projections, Chris would walk over to where she was sitting at a table near the bar, he would sit down opposite her and take her hands, in rapt silence — dreams don't often become reality. And the scene would replay ad nauseam until I shook myself out of it to avoid howling with pain.

Evening comes. I suggest to Chris that we should eat at Chez Tony, a local restaurant we use regularly, there's nothing in the fridge. "Do you want me to go get pizza?" he asks, putting his arms around me — his belly against my back, his mouth in my hair.

I say no, it's a beautiful evening, it would be nice to sit out on the terrace. Hidden under the paperwork on my desk, I've already prepared Claire Antunes's text on my secret phone, I need only press Send, I could still choose not to, but I do it. Then I close the front door and summon the elevator. We go down, walk to the restaurant, he has his arm around my waist, we sit down, look at the menu. Chris doesn't check his phone, maybe he didn't hear the text alert, or, more likely, he's savoring this moment, not expecting anyone or anything, he looks relaxed. I can't take it anymore, every inch of me is trembling on the inside, my stomach is churning with impatience to see what he really is, what I am to him, what I am. The mechanism has been set in motion, that same old fear resurfaces, the fear of not being the love object. It's not me, it's the other woman: that's what I've always thought, always. One of La Rochefoucauld's maxims comes to mind, one that I'd set as an essay topic for my students: "In friendship as in love, we are often made happier by the things we don't know than by those we do." It's probably true. But it's now too late not to know; any second now I'll know.

"What time is it?" I ask. "Maybe we have time for a movie afterward?"

He doesn't reply, he's studying the wine menu, a smile hovering on his lips.

"Can you have a look?" I say, gesturing to his jeans pocket. "I don't have any battery."

With his eyes still on the menu, Chris takes out his phone, opens it almost in slow motion, glances at it, freezes, frowns.

"Eight forty-two." His voice is slightly strangulated, or am I the one who's short of breath? He reads the text, and now his eyes are wavering too, not sure where to look.

This hurts.

"Would you mind going to the tobacconist? I feel like having a cigarette," I say to escape the suffering caused by the sight of him — make him go, make him leave, spare me the spectacle of his indecision!

He stands up like an automaton, stammers, "Yes, yeah, I'll go," puts a hand on my shoulder — such a strong, brusque hand, such a contrast to the sweet sensation it gives me. Through the opening in his shirt I can see the delicate skin of his neck, the crook where I like to rest my lips, I'd like to do that once more before he goes but he's already walking away.

"I'll be back," he says.

The waiter comes over, I order a carafe of rosé. When the waiter brings it I fill both our glasses. I take little sips from mine, my eyes pinned on his.

"I'll be back."

That's where Claire's — Madame Millecam's — novel ends. Or at least the section written in one sitting. Because there's more in the notebook, as you can see, but after several blank pages, as if to mark the passage of time, and it's in a different pen and more uneven handwriting. There are lots of crossings-out, unlike the first section. Some paragraphs have been scrapped, completely blackened with felt-tip pen, others are merely legible jottings. Most likely Claire struggled to decide on an ending: she'd been so open to the different possible outcomes, done so much dreaming and dreading and fantasizing about her love, her jealousy, her desire and her doubts, that it was probably difficult for her to deign to give it a real ending, that is to say a single ending. Mind you, a film screenplay could easily stop right there—and so could a novel actually: she stays sitting at the restaurant table, holding her glass of rosé. The last shot is cut just before she starts drinking the other glass, or perhaps just after, either could work. The waiting, the despair, and the passing time are measured by the contents of those glasses. Unless you opt for a happy ending where we see him coming back around the end of the street, walking toward her as the final credits roll to Patti Smith's "Because the Night Belongs to Lovers," or that other song she loved and sometimes played to me on her iPod during our sessions, "One Day Baby We'll Be Old."

But I'll read you the end as Claire eventually wrote it—Claire or someone else, I'm not really sure, the writing looks slightly different. It's interesting because we hear the man's point of view. It's Chris who narrates the final section. And given what's gone before, this ending isn't without logic, you'll see why. For me, it was this ending that made me do what I did. So listen—just a couple more minutes.

I didn't know what to do when I read that text. Ever asked me to go buy some smokes, which was convenient, I needed to get my head straight. I walked to the end of the street like a zombie, then I checked Claire on Facebook. Her wall hadn't changed, the last posts were several months old: a photo of Portugal like something from a tourist brochure, really moronic, and that was all. I skimmed through some of our old conversations on Facebook, my legs felt wobbly. Seeing her photo again definitely had an effect on me: that luminous unambiguous beauty, the smile on those plump lips, her perfect teeth, her long dark hair gleaming silkily. And her rounded breasts outlined under her sensible sweater. She could have been a model. The sort of girl every guy dreams of, the perfect trophy girl. The shop was closed, I could have bought cigarettes from the Brasserie Georges but that was a long way, Ever would be waiting.

So I went up to the apartment, I'd have to be seriously unlucky not to find a few Camels lying around there. I found an old packet in the key tray by the door. I sat down for a couple of minutes to think. What was I going to say to Claire? Tell her to get lost by text? That wasn't very classy. But then her melodramatic comeback wasn't exactly stylish either. What did she think? That I'd turned to stone, become a statue to eternal love when we had never even met?! Dream on, sweetheart! I didn't know what to say. "Sorry, Claire, I'm living with someone. Her name's Claire too." Or just "So sorry, I'm not in Paris." Or simply, "Welcome to France. Good luck, Claire. Bye." Or nothing. Nada. No reply. Fuggedaboutit. While I sat there slumped on the sofa thinking about it, gazing at Ever's little tartan slippers left under the table, as per usual, I thought back over our weird relationship, Claire's and mine. She must be a bit crazy to issue that sort of ultimatum when she doesn't know me. But I liked that, I had to admit. The impulsiveness, the follow-your-instincts approach, overcoming her own scruples, burning her bridges, basically. It was crazy, unreasonable — very like a woman, no?! A far cry from my steady humdrum life, which was sometimes so boring. I couldn't end up like this, in the silence of cozy domesticity. I had to talk to her, explain things to her. She didn't want me to call, she wanted me to be there: but I didn't have to obey her, I could play this whichever way I liked. Okay, so there was a slight risk I'd be bewitched all over again by her voice, because I remembered the hold it had over me in its day. In its day…it was so long ago already. Ever had filled the void, right away, and her love had won mine over — at least, I had a good life with her. And yet I couldn't make up my mind to go back to her at the restaurant. I needed to talk to Claire first.

I looked at my phone for another minute, staring blankly like an idiot — I was concentrating on what I was going to tell her, or the message I would leave her if, as I thought (or hoped?), she didn't pick up — and I eventually dialed her number. The phone rang once, twice, three times, after the fourth ring I hung up, my heart pounding, and I didn't leave a message after the robotic voice. It wasn't fear that stopped me but the incomprehensible fact that I could hear those rings not only on my phone but also, in exactly the same way and at the same time, in the apartment. I was so stunned by the coincidence that I immediately called Claire back again. Undeniable proof: it was ringing. There was a phone ringing in Ever's bedroom.

By following the sound, I very soon came across a cheap little device I'd never seen in Ever's hands, she only used her iPhone. I flipped it open with a feeling that something catastrophic was happening: this simple action would blow up in my face, I was sure of it, I'd just unearthed the explosive truth.

The texts I'd exchanged with Claire Antunes, the photos I'd sent her…they were all there. I scrolled frantically on the tiny keyboard but my torpedoed brain couldn't come up with a realistic explanation. Had Ever pirated my phone and copied my texts? This woman I trusted so completely. But no, no, because the number on this phone, this fucking phone was Claire Antunes's number. And in the contacts list I was now opening there was only one person: me. Only one number: mine. I pressed the button to listen to voicemail and just stood there, hanging in the emptiness of the bedroom like an unmatched sock on a washing line: my own voice, my voice as a pathetic dick (all mealy-mouthed, honeyed, miserable) whispered inane garbage in my ear, plans, regrets, promises. I sounded so stupid, no, I *was*.

I stood there poleaxed for a good five minutes, my head spinning, before vaguely getting the hoax. It was so twisted that I couldn't make the connection with Ever, who was so straight, so honorable. As well as feeling disbelief, mingled with an aftertaste of humiliation, there was a degree of admiration. Women, all of them, suddenly seemed to me to be a superior species, completely unknowable, spectacular, in a way. And in another way, totally out to lunch. Why the need for this whole circus?

Jealousy. Women's morbid jealousy.

That didn't explain everything, far from it, but it brought an end to any painful questions as to the part that (without even realizing it) I'd been playing for all this time in this obscure scenario. Jealousy is love. Love is an explanation that offers some relief. After the initial disbelief, another question needed answering: What was supposed to happen next in this ambush? I wasn't meant to discover the tangle of lies, what was I supposed to do? Go back and sit down at the table as if nothing had happened and drink a glass of rosé with her? (Her victory.) Or go meet Claire Antunes at Bastille and…and what? Ever had probably planned to turn up herself and gloat at my amazement and shame, before ranting about my unfaithfulness, even if it was virtual, or bludgeoning me with insults. I was torn between fury and laughter, but mostly I had to accept one thing…and Ever's smile, beaming at me from the photo of us hanging over her desk, was no consolation for the fact that was now so blindingly obvious: Claire Antunes didn't exist. That angel was just a fake, my dream in avatar form; I'd been in love with thin air. The physical, organic sensation of being manipulated made me want to see this through to the end. At least I could keep the tangle going a bit longer and make her really suffer. What a monster she was, toying with her own fear after toying with me. I was lost, I didn't know whether I admired her or despised her, whether her craziness thrilled me or disgusted me.

I jumped to my feet, grabbed a travel bag, and stuffed some clothes and all my photo equipment into it, leaving my bedroom conspicuously empty. A real departure or a setup? I didn't know myself. It was nearly nine o'clock. Before I left, I erased all trace of my two calls from her cell phone.

She was drinking a glass of rosé on the terrace at Chez Tony, sitting half turned away so that I had only a fleeting view of her profile, which looked sad: the carafe was almost empty. I continued on my way, making sure she didn't see me, and almost ran to the Café Français. I still loved her, but who?

So now I'm sitting at the Café Français, drinking a pastis, looking out over the square, the cars, the buses. I should take a picture to immortalize the moment — the mortal moment. What if Ever doesn't show up? What am I doing here with my bag packed if Ever doesn't show, if the breakup has already happened? Will I sleep at my parents' place in Sevran tonight, and drink coffee with Mom tomorrow morning and she'll ask me why I always mess everything up? No, no, and no again, I want her to come, I want to make her pay for this perverse game. She loves me, I'm going to act incredibly cold before taking her in my arms — maybe. It'll depend on her smile, I'm not her slave either. Memories come back to me, the past scrolling by as if I've had an accident. How did she hatch such a twisted plot? Inventing a life, inventing Gilles, inventing Portugal, inventing the impossible? Why did she need...

That's when I saw her. It was like an apparition. I turned around, looking for the waiter, to ask for another one, and there she was. All in black, her brown hair pulled back, a sad expression, but it's her, I recognize her. My heart races, I don't understand anything, but what a lot of anything! She's a way off but we make eye contact. She looks at me, then looks away, with no change of expression, her eyes simply moving on to something else. This is all so confusing, I'm not designed for so much emotion, for so many enigmas. My chest is like a jigsaw puzzle threatening to explode.

So I stood up, walked over to her table, and put my bag down on it. Claire? I asked almost sharply. She looked up, her mouth half open, her skin lustrous, her eyes look surprised, hovering on the brink of a smile, she does something adorable with one eyebrow, raising it slightly. My name's Katia, she says.

And that's it. The end of the notebook. Strange, isn't it? A document, but so much more. So how to explain? When I finished reading this, it seemed obvious to me that this woman's life, well, this patient's life, was dominated by guilt. Guilt so all-consuming that even when she imagined how the story could have been written differently and afforded her some happiness in real life, she came up with a sad ending, inflicting punishment on herself, leaving her alone with her remorse. Her pathology incontrovertibly derives from pronounced hysteria as presented in the definition we all know: a desire for dissatisfaction. It *had* to fail, that's how this story could be summarized. I won't insult you by reminding you how important masochism is to numerous subjects, particularly women—my own thesis was about "Destructiveness and the Death Wish in Women's Neuroses." In Claire's case, in Madame Millecam's case, well, in her novel, we could even go so far as to say there is a desperate quest for a "catastrophic moment," a willful search for proof of her inability to be loved, I would readily call this a "disaster craving." It is probably coupled with an unconscious desire to atone for something, to self-flagellate. Her niece's suicide (which she refutes in her novel because it's so unbearable for her) is clearly a factor in this—she punishes herself for failing to protect Katia despite the promise she made her brother—but her guilt is most likely rooted further back in the past: a repressed childhood incident, maternal postnatal depression, wishing someone in her family were dead, what do I know?

Nevertheless—and this is where you certainly can direct the blame at me—instead of helping her delve through her childhood to find out what it was that kept her in this depressive, guilty frame of mind for three years, switching from aggression to passivity and in a state of near aboulia, instead of doing that, I decided to try to find something in real life to extricate her from her isolation—her internment: to get her out of here. She reminded me of Roger, a patient I met when I was training at the Clinique des Ormeaux in Blois. He'd been running the beekeeping workshops for twenty years, it was all he did, tending the hives, harvesting the honey, planning to rear new queens...As my mentor, Dr. Aury, pointed out at the time, he'd turned into a bee. Well, it was rather like that for Claire: she'd turned into waiting. She waited, it took up all her time: waiting. What was she waiting for? Nothing, that's just the point. Was she waiting for a dead man, for him to come back, waiting for love, for it to come along, waiting for forgiveness? To be allowed it? Perhaps. But it's more likely she was waiting for nothing. It wasn't negative, that's not a negative statement, even if it is less objectively productive than tending bees. Waiting had become her whole persona, the waiting had dissolved the object of the wait. She had turned to stone in that state, one two three eternal sunshine, Penelope without the suitors, Penelope without a returning Ulysses, but who still doggedly unpicks whatever sort of life she may be living.

When I started the inquiry about which you've been given information, my sole objective was to find her an escape route, to remove the burden of her crushing guilt, to set her in motion again, so that she could at least get out of this terrifying freeze-frame. Besides, I intuitively felt, and what happened next proved I was right on this point, I felt events hadn't actually happened as she said. I knew that she first arrived here distraught and rambling after a serious decompensation, then returned after each discharge prey to renewed bouts of delirium—I'd read the reports. At first I thought she might be lying, fictionalizing from the start, inventing everything she said—to hide something else, or maintain control. Because she tries to control everything, using lies or laughter. My predecessor made a note of her fondness for fiction and amusing stories—stories in general. She likes telling stories. In fact he pointed out the difference, in what she related, between irony, which can hurt or destroy, and humor, which is a vital restorative force. Our patient is very good at using both, attacking or relaxing her listener, but it's always a way of protecting herself. Jokes keep reality at arm's length, irony tackles tragedy but also keeps it at bay, she uses her wit to survive. Or otherwise she invents, fabricates. Her idea of freedom is to be brilliant, and fables are her way of escaping unadulterated madness. A sort of organized delirium, you see. But it doesn't matter whether or not it's true. What matters is her saying it. Or believing it.

Anyway, one way or another, whether she was doing it deliberately or not, I thought there was something strange about this story: Chris, the Internet womanizer, the hustler who was used to plenty of action, committing suicide for a girl he's only seen in photos...I know that sort of thing happens, that you can die because something doesn't happen, that psychotic decompensation is always a possibility, that there are little boys lost inside grown men, that grandmas are really still little girls, but to go that far? It just didn't feel right to me. Something didn't fit. I didn't believe it. Yes, he'd gone off-radar. There was no trace of him on the Internet, particularly as Claire had never known his family name, only his first name, Christophe, and his Facebook name, KissChris—it's extraordinary when you come to think of it, a relationship between two pseudonyms: like something in a novel, in fact, fictional creations.

So I decided to track down Joe, the only apparent witness to the whole story, in order to shed some light on what happened. I wanted to know, I have to admit, there was an element of pure curiosity—about human resourcefulness, human logic, human beings. What Claire had told me about Joe painted a classic picture of narcissistic perversion, and I was right about that. I managed, with what was an apparently casual question and without disclosing any of my plans to Claire, to get Joe's family name from her. He wasn't in the phone directory. I knew he had a house in Lacanau, I'm sure I could have found him that way, but I did something easier: I looked for him on Facebook. And there he was. I contacted him via private messaging, saying I was Claire's doctor and I'd like to meet him. He agreed.

I'll spare you the details, you've read the transcripts I made of our conversations. There are instantly recognizable signs of the complete emotional indifference of a narcissist, but also a degree of naive pride in his successful manipulations. He admitted almost immediately that Chris wasn't dead, that he'd invented the whole thing as revenge for Claire's "betrayal." What betrayal? I asked.

"Trying to pick up my buddy when we were together. One evening I recognized her voice in a message she'd left for Chris, those mannered intonations, the fucking idiot wanted me to listen to it too so I could savor the smooth sound of her voice. *Claire Antunes?* My ass! Fucked up, yes! Bitch! I didn't say anything to Chris, how was that going to make me look? I'm not some guy who gets cheated on, no way; but revenge is a dish best eaten cold. What a whore! And what's she up to now? Are you doing her, is that what's going on? She wants them younger and younger! So she didn't die of a broken heart, then? Ah, ah! I'd've been surprised! I could see she took it hard when I fed her that red herring. But she didn't wait long before finding herself some consolation, from what I can see. I tried to track her down a year ago—I'm the sentimental type! No, I'm kidding, I thought I'd do her again, she's still pretty good for her age, isn't she?—but she'd gone out of circulation: she wasn't on Facebook, there was no answer on her number, she'd stopped teaching at the university, she'd moved…I even went and stood outside her ex's house one time (the guy remarried, by the way, a real bombshell, a brunette with these tits, I can't tell you). I saw her kids, that pair of brats. But no sign of her. Well, I gave up. So how is she, how is the bimbo? You're her doctor? So she's sick? She doesn't have AIDS, does she?"

I didn't reply, in my personal capacity I had to restrain myself from punching him, I have to say. I asked him about Chris. Joe said evasively that he was no longer in touch with him. That after "Claire Antunes" defected, going off to get married in Portugal, Chris was a bit depressed, so Joe recommended he change his Facebook profile, shake himself up a bit, which he did. Christophe—KissChris—just turned into Toph. Joe discreetly blocked Claire's number on Chris's phone, just in case. "Undesirable," that's what she'd become, "and the bitch deserved it," he told me. Then the two of them went to Mexico on a reportage Joe had managed to find, and Chris met a girl out there. Joe and he fell out over money, Joe came home alone and it was then that he saw Claire again and announced the invented suicide.

Joe asked me where Claire was living now, and obviously I didn't tell him that thanks to him, she's been wasting away in a psychiatric clinic for three years. I didn't want to give him the satisfaction.

I went home completely dazed, but I had what I wanted. Just to be sure, I looked for Toph on Facebook. Not being a "friend," I didn't have access to much, but there was a picture of a man of about forty with auburn hair, a photographer born in Sevran, living in Mexico City, with a signature that ended in a little flower. A father of one.

That was when I made my second mistake, I know. I showed a lack of judgment, or of professional lucidity. I thought that truthfulness would have a beneficial effect on this patient. That by drawing her out of the imaginary world that was destroying her, by showing her she'd been manipulated, that *she* was the victim—she hadn't killed anyone, she was the one who'd been killed—I'd be helping her, rescuing her, even. I wanted to save her.

I don't know. Maybe. You couldn't call it countertransference because she didn't transfer much onto me, I don't think. But I probably failed to take advice, to refer to one of you. I entered into an interpersonal relationship with her.

Love? I don't know. Either way, I wanted her to start loving again. Me or someone else. Someone else...or me.

The opposite happened. I thought I was bringing her fresh hope: no one had died for her. And I brought her despair: no one had died for her. I realized too late that this death was what was keeping her alive. This tragic passion justified her existence: she'd been loved to distraction, to destruction. Deep down, she was living here, at La Forche, only so she could continue to live with this love. A psychiatric clinic is the perfect place for her, the place to be: the mad are the same species as those who are in love, we even say "madly in love." There was no one here to disturb her morbid enjoyment. Her tragedy was glorious. She spoke to me so readily in our interviews for the sheer pleasure of staying in the story. And I destroyed everything. I thought the truth would bring her back to life. But not everyone is ready for the truth. People couldn't give a damn about it, the truth, I mean. What matters is what they believe. They write over the truth. They make it disappear with all their fabrications and narratives. And they live off that, off the stories they tell. Their lives are a palimpsest. No point trying to see what's underneath. Meanwhile, we psychiatrists claim to want the truth. That's garbage. A psychiatric hospital is the very opposite: it protects from the truth.

Her face when I showed her Toph's profile on my cell...a terrible memory. I understood right then, in that fraction of a second, that I was wrong, it was a disaster. She recognized him, I saw the look in her eyes when she identified him. Her world fell apart, she slid off her chair, and as she collapsed to the floor, she just said, "The shame." I don't know whether she was talking about herself, Chris, or Joe. Or possibly me. Because I was ashamed, it's true. That's all I can say. I'm ashamed and I'm suffering. The pervert is actually me, by all accounts. But I didn't want this, oh no, I didn't want it.

Afterward she had her really acute episodes, she hallucinated, hallucinating the world. She hallucinated to stay alive. But dying is a higher power. And I didn't know she wasn't taking her medication, that she was stockpiling it and hiding it at the foot of the fig tree.

Do what you want with me. I want only one thing: for her to live. For her to get out of this.

No.

Yes.

Yes.

Perhaps. Perhaps I do love her, yes, after all, yes, why not use the right word. I love her. She moves me. I want to take her in my arms. I think about her, I carry her in my heart, I cradle her in my memory. She touches me and captivates me, yes, I'm a captive. I want to see her. "Love is being there." There is no other truth. And I like being there for her. I'd like to bandage her wounds. She may be mad, after all, in the way we understand the word. Certainly. But it's the mad who heal us, isn't it?

II

a personal story

The only way out of a personal story is to write it.
— MARGUERITE DURAS

I tell you this true story just to prove that I can.
My frailty has not yet reached a point
at which I can no longer tell a true story.
— JOAN DIDION

3

ROUGH DRAFT OF A LETTER TO LOUIS O.

My dear Louis,

Sorry for this handwritten letter, I don't have a computer at the moment, I hope you'll be able to read it.

Your message upset me. I can understand that you don't like my title, even if I disagree. You think *Go Die!* is too aggressive for a cover? Too cheap? Even if I add a couplet from Corneille as an epigraph? Are you saying it's as if I'm addressing readers, as if I'm rejecting them before they even start? Fine. I don't think readers take titles personally, not at all, it certainly never occurs to me, but I'll accept that—from a commercial point of view—you may be right, I don't know, we'll talk about this again, that's not the most important thing. I'm far more concerned about the rest—what you say after that, about the content: that, given the situation in publishing over the last few years, it's best to be cautious. You ask so many questions. Are you like all the rest, then? You're afraid. You don't want any trouble, you're remembering recent novels whose authors have been sued, and their publishers along with them, you've lost a couple of court cases yourself. Once bitten, twice shy, you say.

First let me remind you you've won some too. Literature sometimes triumphs. "The fact that the events related were experienced by the author detracts nothing from the aesthetic dimension of the work"—don't you find that reassuring? Mostly I'm sad that my editor—my friend—doesn't have more faith in me. How can you think, you, Louis, that there's no distance between fiction and reality? Or worse: that I stole this story from someone? Parasitized their life? Don't you know what writing is? You've been an editor for fifty years and you don't understand writers? We've been friends for twenty years, you've read all my books, and you want a lawyer to read *Go Die!*? Are you afraid someone will recognize themselves, is that it? We're co-owners of our lives and that worries you? Are you wondering exactly how far the communal parts extend? You're probably thinking that while I was in residence for a writing workshop in a psychiatric hospital, I milked the tragic experiences of an inmate. Is that it? Don't you trust me? Do you think I'm completely unethical?

You're right, in a way, but not the way you think. I'm a coward, that's true. I don't have the moral courage it would take to tell the precise truth—the naked truth, which is one hell of a cuckold. A banal experience I had—pitiful thing, a cuckold—a micro-event but I got lost in it. I don't have the courage because it's too stupid, too vulgar, too insignificant, because as a woman, as a writer, as a woman writer, I'd look like an idiot, a pathetic girl, seriously neurotic. Hence the novel, the manuscript you've just read. Pure fiction—or nearly—even though the clinic really does exist and I'm still running a writing workshop there. But because you have your doubts, and in order to reassure you, you and Mr. Thingy, your lawyer, I'll tell you the real story, the true story,

the one that happened to me. You should like this off-camera
stuff, you, as an editor, you'll see, it's closely connected with
writing itself, with literature. "True confessions," that's what
we could call this. ~~And you're bound to like seeing me in the
miserable part I play, secretly you'll enjoy it, although you'd
never admit that, it might even move you: I've noticed how
much you gays like mature women frantically scrabbling
toward their own destruction. Your idols are all aging and
suicidal, they die listening to a Dalida song. What it is that
so fascinates you, I don't know: the fact you see yourself in it
or that you hate yourself in it?~~

Above all, I hope to reassure you: in the novel you've
just read I changed, or at least I could change, most of the
names, places, and professions. Anyway, a photographer will
fire the reader's imagination better than a musician. In fact
he was a singer-songwriter with dreams of releasing a single,
having a song in the top ten, and I was meant to write the
lyrics. But to avoid worrying you, I'll keep the identities fictional, it'll be easier, particularly as the whole opening of my
story is pretty much identical, so you need only reread up to
page 56. Like my character, I created a false Facebook page
and played an undercover game with—let's call him Joe. It
was very immature of me, I'll agree. Age is a strictly administrative concept, you know. And novelists have the right
to inhabit novels in real life. Anyway, if that's what's worrying you, I don't think setting up a fake Facebook account is
enough for anyone to file a complaint. Mind you, if it were,
you'd have to charge the tens of thousands, no, hundreds
of thousands of people all over the world on every dating
site and social network who pass themselves off as someone

they're not, changing their age, lying about their work, their marital status, even their sex, posting photos that are twenty years old and inventing a life that's freer and more exciting than their own. You wouldn't believe how many people invent a character for themselves! Life's a novel. Did you know there's an Internet site that helps people construct another life for themselves? Not a video game or a Second Life but IRL, in real life. It provides tangible proof of the things you invent, alibis for the little lies you tell people, theater tickets for plays you've never seen, hotel reservations in a country you've never visited, a detailed report of a conference you didn't attend, pictures of you in a Chinese newspaper dated the day you were in Pornic with your secretary for the weekend, fake photos, fake qualifications, fake memories, and fake proof of your fake life. Compared to that I'm the Care Bears. Who's the injured party? There's no adultery, no fraud. I haven't taken anyone's identity, as you'll see, I've just invented one. My deception doesn't do anyone any harm, except me. Besides, Chris did so much lying himself in this whole affair that I can't really see him firing off about the imposture. In the ongoing fictions of our lives, in our lies and our accommodations with the truth, in our need to possess, dominate, and control other people, we're all novelists in the making. We all invent our lives. The difference, in my case, is that I'm living the life I invented. And, like every creation, it's broken free of its creator. If you want to be difficult you could say I'm living it only so that I can write it, that this life is only a pretext for writing. But it's completely the other way around. Life is beyond me, it destroys me, writing is just a way of surviving it—the only way. I don't live to write, I write to survive life. I'm saving myself. Writing a novel for yourself is like building an asylum.

So, for the reasons I've told you, I forged an avatar for myself, created my character, Claire Antunes. (Incidentally, don't fret, the pretty brunette really was a picture chosen at random on Google Images, and sent only by private messaging—stay cool, lawyer guy, no litigation on that front. And anyway I don't have any nieces.) That crazy little Claire lived her life through me, I hadn't anticipated it at all, she fell in love, I really had to do something about it. And, despite this love, I was more lucid than she was, or more cynical, at least I thought I was, not so misty-eyed, more beady-eyed, I was up for the poker game, prepared to gamble in order to see. I was like a reader halfway through a crime thriller, dying to know what happened next. And, as you know, I loathe anything virtual, it makes me very anxious, the things that don't happen frighten me far more than those that do, I need to feel the world around me. So I wanted to meet Chris for real—IRL. I, Camille, I'm more ballsy or more confident than Claire, more hotheaded than my alter ego, not so preoccupied with youth and aging, I couldn't pass up the chance. Not that I would turn my back on the dream, quite the opposite, I spend my life dreaming, I write all my books in a dream; chaos in a bubble, the antechamber to the book, that's my greatest pleasure. But I also like actually getting down to it, concretely, pen to paper, skin and bone. I dream of things happening. Then, in order to make them happen—whether it's writing or loving, and whatever the cost, the price I'll have to pay, I never think about that—I'm ready for action. Well, I was.

At first I tried to meet Chris "by chance," and I went to wait at the Gare de l'E at Montparnasse Station (don't worry, there isn't really a house in Lacanau). But his father was there. All I managed to do was confirm how strong my feelings were for him. There was something dazzling about Chris, like the sun, he saturated the screen of reality, he had an imposing presence—and there he was on that station platform somehow looking as lost as an evacuated orphan. Because at the same time his vulnerability smacked you in the face, I thought he was in a bad way. Precarious—that's the first word that came to me when I saw him: a precarious man. Do you know the etymology of the word "precarious"? Obtained by prayer. Except that I had to find another way, I wasn't going down on my knees to beg him to love me! What I do know is that when I saw him, I wanted him. Mind you, at over forty (I changed the ages too, you saw that, his and mine—I thought that in a novel it's like being in a film or on Meetic: it's best for the heroine to be on the right side of the expiration date), at over forty, then, he still behaved like a teenager: his clothes, his unkempt hair, his guitar slung across his back, his daddy. But maybe that was what made him attractive, that refusal to bow to time, it hit a nerve in me. And it was the start of the summer, people were leaving Paris, I couldn't seem to write much, Joe had left me high and dry, my daughters were far away, I needed a life-giving source, proof of life. Chris was like a promise just waiting to be kept, I remembered the gentleness in his voice on the phone, and in my daydreams that became confused with the unknown gentleness of his hands. I knew, because Chris had told me himself, he didn't have any money. Just seeing his father would have told me that: the stooped outline, the hunched back, the restrained greeting, the muddy color of his face under his cap—a total contrast to what life must have been like in Lacanau with Joe. So I chose a solution that had the advantage of doing Chris a favor. Because, to be honest, I felt guilty about the little game I'd been playing with him for months, falsely stringing him along—no, not falsely, that's not the right word—stringing him along with a hidden love. I was the cause of the sadness I could see in his face. I'd run away, claiming I was marrying another man in Lisbon, leaving all his hopes dashed. He was moping about a phantom I'd cobbled together. It seemed only natural I should *pay*. I even pictured nothing happening between us, never meeting him, just that I would pay my dues, find my own way to reimburse the debt of love he'd spent in vain on me.

So I messaged him from my real Facebook account, the one belonging to Camille, the writer, Camilleon to my nearest and dearest (yes, I know, Louis, I can see your smile. But this went way beyond the boundaries: the chameleon was struggling on a tartan blanket). I introduced myself straight out: so I was a former friend of Joe's, back in the day Joe had shown me his pictures and I thought they were beautiful, I particularly remembered one: an arrow drawn onto the ground with the sign TO HAPPINESS. I was looking for an original idea for a gift and wanted to give the image to a girlfriend for her birthday, was it for sale? I gave him my phone number and a friend request. He called me soon. I was afraid he'd recognize my voice, the voice of Claire Antunes, with whom he'd had long conversations so many evenings, so I said hello in a deep voice. Yes, he sold his pictures. Two hundred euros each. "What size is that?" I asked.

He laughed smugly. "No size. At that price, I'll email it to you and you can have it printed, and framed if you like. I'm the artist, I sell the work of art, I don't supply the materials." I was speechless with surprise: was this the same man who, three weeks earlier, begged me in his tender, modest voice not to forget him? Confronted with this silence at my end, he softened. "If you like I can sell you the print from my last exhibition, it's a hundred centimeters by two hundred and mounted on a metal plate. But then that's three hundred euros. So you're a friend of Joe's? I have to tell you, we had a bust-up, big time, we don't talk anymore, I'm sorry but he's such an asshole."

I said quickly that I didn't see Joe anymore either. "But you and I have talked before," I added facetiously (quick, quick, keep this going). "Yes, one time I called Joe and he handed the phone to you, you weren't very nice, you said: 'Go die!' So you see, we know each other."

I laughed but Chris took offense, "No, surely not, you're making this up. I'm not like Joe, I know how to behave."

I just said, "Maybe." It wasn't the time to spoil the conversation. He doesn't know himself, I thought, he doesn't know himself at all. There are people like that, who really don't know who they are, they're a million miles from recognizing themselves—it's a slow process seeing yourself, some never do. Then I thought that perhaps I really was the one who'd got it wrong, that it hadn't been Chris with Joe that evening, it wasn't like him.

He said he was living in Sevran but often came to Paris. "I'm taking my cousin to the airport next week, and staying in his apartment near the Porte des Lilas while he's away. If you like we could have a drink and I can give you the photo. Then you can pay me cash, which is better."

I said "Okay" and he said "Cool."

He was already there when I arrived, leaning against a post at the mouth of the Métro station. I'd almost canceled the whole thing, my intuition was saying nothing I wanted to hear. The Prince Charming on the phone had sounded just like an evil toad, so many virtual relationships fizzle out. But when I saw him, I got the same vibes as at the station: he was handsome, nonchalant, anxious too, and not quite hiding it. And all the longing accumulated by Claire Antunes during that loving correspondence couldn't be reabsorbed that quickly. The craving to touch him, smell him, make him love me had flourished independently, like a plant, it would take more than vague disappointment to pull it out by the roots. And also I'm a writer, human beings are my raw material. I have no limits in that department, you know that, Louis, I'm infinitely curious. I arm-wrestle with people's passions. I always think I'm strong enough to stir up the molten magma, and all I could see here was something vaguely like barely glowing embers. I should have paid more attention to the familiar feeling of anxiety that goes hand in hand with the beginnings of love, a feeling that seems to be warning me of imminent danger: a sort of cement that hardens in my chest till it hurts, hampering my breathing, and for no obvious reason, as if I were missing some vital thing that I've never actually had. For me, the first manifestations of desire come in the shape of anticipated pain, of grief in advance, as if my whole body were reminding me it's going to fail—even if it happens it'll fail because it's already failed, it's written in the air we breathe, and on the wall, across the city, everywhere, the already mummified body of love. But when I'm given this internal warning I don't run away, quite the opposite, usually—at least if I'm in public—I extricate myself with excessive poise, small talk plays the part of adrenaline for me when there's some life-threatening risk, I overplay my sociability, don't give silence a chance, let alone the distress calls of my inner animal, I concentrate on appearing unaffected by all assaults, the beast howls unheard, my smile is a mask, I block every exit, I shore myself up to the death, I melt into the landscape, camouflaged on every level, not for nothing am I a chameleon.

That's what I did at the mouth of the Métro station that evening, even though Claire Antunes's chest was very much there, palpitating with desire and fear. We kissed on the cheek and headed off in search of a bar. I was secretly aroused, finding myself by his side like this when we'd been flirting on Facebook for months—and here's something you may not know, Louis, the word "flirt" comes from the Old French *fleureter*, to exchange little flowers. Well, that's exactly what we'd been doing till then, when he posted pictures of lotus flowers and daisies for me, rose-tinted stuff for the little wild-flower he thought I was. He didn't suspect a thing, of course, and how could he? He'd have actually needed to listen to my voice, to pay attention to me, to *recognize* me.

"So you're a writer, then?" he asked once we were sitting at the terrace of a Moorish café. "What do you write?" "Yes," I started to say, "I—" "Your scarf's real cool," he said to the girl at the next table, a sassy brunette who smiled at him and glanced at me hesitantly. "I mostly write novels, but also some—" "You should wear red, it would really suit you, you can trust me, I'm a photographer, I have the eye." "Oh, you're a photographer," the brunette replied, interested. "I'm an actor, and you live…" She looked at me, not sure whether to include me in that "you." "…You live around here?" "Yeah, just around the corner. And you?" "Yes, I'm rooming with a girlfriend in that building over there, at the end of the street." "Are you a stage or film actor?" I asked, perusing her with my chameleon eyes that were not about to settle for being the color of the background wall. "Mostly stage," she said, smiling, "but I dream of doing movies." I moved my chair closer to hers. "And are you working at the moment? I'm a writer, I'd like to write for the theater." Now deposed, Chris had already turned his attention to a group of young guys playing cards at another table. "Hey, Rasta," he called to one of them, "I love your look, are you an artist? If you ever need photos, here's my card. I'll take a coupl'a shots, you don't mind, do you?" He produced his camera and, not waiting for an answer, took a few pictures of the group, then he suddenly snapped several of me without warning. "Hey, stop!" I said, forcing a laugh (you know how I hate having my photo taken, Louis), "what about my photo rights?" He looked at his screen, scrolling through the images, and didn't even look up as he said, "Chill, I'll delete them, they're all terrible, anyway." After a second Kir, I made as if to get up and leave. "Wait," he said, taking my hand, "are you hungry? We're going to go eat, aren't we?" And before I could answer he was leading me off down the street. We walked hand in hand till we came to a restaurant. "Do you have someone?" he asked me in the same voice he might use to ask if I had any cigarettes. I said, "No," I said. "And you?" He let go of my hand. "Here, this place is good," he announced. He sat down at an outside table next to a group of Canadian tourists and started handing out his business cards again. He took contact details from a girl who claimed she was an artists' agent or wanted to be one, I wasn't too sure in all the commotion. The young man next to me asked me what I did in life, I said I was a writer, he was very interested and asked a lot of questions. A Pakistani man selling roses offered a bouquet to Chris, who brushed him aside with a flick of his hand, the man persisted, putting the flowers in my arms. "God, this is such a pain," Chris said, "everyone thinks we're together, it's crazy…" He ate quickly, savagely, satisfying his hunger but with no pleasure. When the time came to pay he went to the restroom, I settled the check. "You shouldn't have," he said when he came back, "by the way, do you have my dough for the photo? In cash?" I handed him the money, he counted it, standing right there in the street. The Canadian tourists watched us, perplexed, sitting there together like that they looked like a mosaic of bafflement. Chris and I went back to the bar, the pretty actor was still there, and she introduced us to her roommate, they were poring over a magazine, taking a personality test based on color preferences. I chose green and white, which meant I was a homebody and I liked money. "Well, well, well," Chris said, his face serious, disapproving, "you're the exact opposite of me." He went on talking well-being and chromology with the girls. "I'm going home," I said, standing up. "Hey, wait," he said quickly, also getting to his feet. I thought he wanted to walk me back, but he stretched, revealing his forearms tattooed with birds, his russet-brown hair glinted amber in the lights. "You disappointed? Didn't you find anyone? How about the Brazilian guy over there? Don't you like him? I think he's looking at you." I turned to look, there was a man dressed in green and yellow, and yes, he seemed to like me, shame he needed to lose a hundred pounds. "Listen, I don't need anyone," I lied. "I'm tired, I'm going home." "Okay, see ya then," Chris said, and he sat back down next to the girls. I walked down the street, I was wearing my African dress, the one that makes people miss me when I'm gone, Joe used to say, it was a good formula, I could feel Chris watching my figure as I walked away, but perhaps it was just me needing to think he was, like a camera lens that didn't turn away immediately. A little farther on two young black guys were sitting on a step with cans of beer, they were listening to rap, turned up too loud. "You're ravishing," one of them said as I passed by, and when I didn't reply but hurried on past he yelled, "Hey, lady, that's a compliment!" So I waved my hand without turning around and said, "Thanks for the compliment." And that's what I thought, I felt gratitude. I was mostly touched—must have been the old teacher in me—by his use of the word "ravishing," I was pleased he'd used this old-fashioned word, keeping it alive in his own way, and going to that trouble for me, well, it felt as if it was for me. This feeling of gratitude kept me going to the Métro; as I went down the steps into Télégraphe Station, so deep underground, my longing for Chris was still a sharp pang, but my shame for feeling this desire was gaining the upper hand, thousands of girls were protesting inside me, a united clamor thrumming in my head: What an asshole! As I continued underground, I soon found I had only one phrase in mind, as if it was tagged on my every internal wall, although I wasn't sure who it was intended for—him, me, Claire Antunes?—but then I knew, and I muttered it with each downward step, feeling better every time I said it to him, freeing myself of his image, his voice, his misleading messages, sinking, burying his memory in that subterranean dungeon, then in the metallic clang, then in the drunken, laughing Saturday night crowds, waving a virtual hand toward his pathetic ghost: "Go die!" I told him.

He called me three days later, apologized for "not being exclusive the other evening." "That's how I am," he added, "I like people." He was calling for two reasons: first, he needed to deliver the picture I'd paid for (I hadn't forgotten, had I? TO HAPPINESS!); but also, he'd had an idea—"We should do a book together." He'd done some research, he hadn't read any of my work, didn't have time, but a friend had told him I was a good writer, and since he was a very good photographer, "it might be cool."

I was going away to the country with my mother, I said yes, maybe, we could talk about this some more another time. I went to the Auvergne region, he called me every day, his voice was there in forests, near beehives, beside streams.

He didn't hear Claire Antunes's voice in mine, but he liked mine, liked listening to it. The idea was to do a book about rural folk: we'd drive off along the back roads of France in "the old girl"—his vintage Citroën—and stop in villages. To get a better understanding of how people live in the country—other people's lives are important—we'd find accommodation in people's homes, staying on farms, in barns. It would look good, too.

"Okay," he said, "so I'm a little scared where all this might take the two of us." I pretended not to hear, or not to understand, he pursued the idea: "In the hay together, just picture it! Not really your style, though. Are you scared too? 125 But do you feel like going on this trip with me? You're bound to be the wrong person but hey…I bet you dreamed about it last night, I can tell you it made me completely…Whoa, what am I saying? Let's just allow life to bestow its blessings on us…"

I sent him pictures of sheep, garbage devoid of all sex appeal, selfies with the local farm laborer, he made teasing remarks about the city chick playing farm girl—I actually know the place like the back of my hand, I've been going there since I was four, my grandfather was born there, I can milk a goat, I've watched cows calve and pigs die, and seen depression kill the winter on the end of a length of rope, I know the rural world far better than he does. But he wasn't listening. He was doing everything he could to charm me on the phone, compliments, double-entendres, plans, promises.

The less I responded to his performance, the more he wound me up; his voice had these shifting modulations, it was very erotic—much more than it had been with Claire

Antunes. But sometimes I got caught up in his game, I played along, and he immediately came back with a sort of condescension—we were just friends, if that, on Facebook, *going away together*, of course not, he'd never said that, what was I thinking? It was as if he couldn't decide which role to play in the conventional carve-up of stereotypes: the man's or the woman's: he displayed either all the characteristics of a bold hunter or all those of the elusive prey that had to be won over with a mighty struggle if you could first break down its impressive indifference. I didn't like this coming and going from one role to the next, because there was no leeway between the two, no flexibility, he was one or the other, two parodies of subject and object, outrageous seducer or rebel resisting seduction, conquering knight or *dame sans merci*. Louis, you need to understand (I can hear you from here), this isn't against you. A woman within a man is fine if it's harmonious, not when it fights to the death. He didn't leave room for complicity, and forced me to be careful what I said, to pretend. How could I capitulate to an appeal that immediately reversed into rejection? How could I take a refusal which would turn back into begging? Whatever I did I was wrong. I thought his mood swings might be due to his recent disappointment in love, which excused and justified his ambivalent wariness of other women. But I didn't feel at liberty to confide in him as Claire Antunes had. I was on a tightrope and I could easily fall, I could tell, although I soon forgot that. And yet—or because of this?—my desire was back, different from the desire I'd felt when I was her, more fretful, the longing to touch him and smell him was less tender, more avid, this urge to let my senses decide which game I should play for which candle.

So when I returned to Paris I agreed to see him. He had hassled me every day I was in the Auvergne to find out when I'd be back, but once I was actually back he was less impatient, and made a date to see me three days later. He was staying near the Porte des Lilas at his cousin's place—"he's an airline steward, he's often out of town," Chris explained, and because he loved his cousin's cat, Daddy, he often came to cat-sit. So that accounted for the pictures of a cat sprawled on a saggy old sofa that he'd posted on Facebook, I'd thought it was at his parents' place in Sevran. He gave me the address and the entry code, "it'll be better than a café for work," he said. I arrived with my MacBook and a lace dress I'd bought the day before, thinking he'd like it; but I wasn't planning on taking the initiative, and I'd prepared for the fact that nothing might happen, like the first time. Let's say I was playing "to see," to give this virtual love a second chance to become real, like starting a book that's going to end up in a drawer. I didn't really believe in it, I even wondered whether he had some kind of problem, but the Claire Antunes in me still hoped, I could feel the energy of her love moving inside me like a baby about to be born.

Chris showed me in. I'd brought a bottle of wine and a packet of pistachio nuts, he took them from me and went off to the kitchen while I walked through to the living room, where I recognized the shapeless sofa. I'd taken an antihistamine, I'm allergic to cats. But for now Daddy was nowhere to be seen.

The window was open onto the evening air, it was warm, there was a tree nearby, its branches reaching toward me. Chris came back empty-handed and sat in a chair to my left. We talked about one thing and another, not even about our vague plans for a book, I found it hard tearing my eyes away from the crook of his neck, hard not to look where Claire Antunes would have wanted to. We didn't have much to say to each other and I started wondering vaguely what the hell I was doing there without even a drink in my hand, when he reached out to me and started stroking me with the tips of his fingers, casually, as you would a cat, while he continued talking. He stroked my breasts, my thighs, my stomach through my dress, gently but in a very sexual way—not my hair or my neck as he would have done with Claire, I thought. I don't remember what he whispered at that point, my name perhaps, or questions about what I like—I let him touch me, my ears burning red. *Is that good?* How can I speak or think, the question's already there, I'm turning to liquid, shapeless, although his hands remind me of the precise shape of my body's every contour. *Tell me, Camille, do you like that?* His deep, authoritative voice is unfamiliar. He takes my hand and puts it over his penis, he has an erection, a wave of heat rises to my hairline, there are no words in my mouth. Claire Antunes is disintegrating, I forget about my dress with its simpering dreams, I'm the one with Chris's body up against mine, and what a body, we're not on Facebook paying each other lip service, our lips have found another service to render, we're here and this is love, love is being there. His erection is my trophy, I stroke it through the fabric of his pants, and unbutton them. A man with an erection is wonderful for a woman, he's her scepter, I wonder whether men know that—oh, okay, Louis, you don't have to answer that one—I find it intoxicating, it's both domination and abdication, the vanishing point of all mistrust, consorting with a stiffened phallus I become both queen and consort.

Then he kissed me, his lips barely rested on mine, his tongue was soft and secretive, slow, his eyes closed, his hands cupping my face, thoughtful, his tenderness melted my heart, he's kissing Claire Antunes, I thought, he wants me but he's kissing Claire Antunes. He stood abruptly, "Come, we're going to another room," and led me by the hand down a corridor toward a bedroom. We stopped on the way there, by the front door, to kiss again. He took off his shirt, his movements slowed by the half-light, I put my hand on his bare shoulder, it was curved like the handle on a shutter, we're immortal, it opened out onto a summer landscape, a fiery shiver of sensations, the world had grown immeasurably, it was expanding between my ribs in a blaze of air that burned everything, we're eternal, it was palpitating in infinite space, nothing existed but us, life's never like this, except in that moment, galloping bareback on a demented horse.

What I want to explain to you, Louis, is that everything that happens next in the story has just one motive, and only one: getting back to that moment. Reliving it. Starting over. Grabbing the demented horse by the mane in all that vertiginous speed that brings tears to the eyes. Nothing else. Virginia Woolf says nothing has happened until you've written about it. That's true of almost everything, but not of being in someone's arms. The clinch clinches it, it's an event. Even if we never talk about it, even if there are no words to describe it and we silence it forever, when we make love, we are, we matter, we're relevant.

"My love," he murmured as he stroked me and kissed me skillfully, slowly, "my love." I said, "Yes, yes," I was his love, I let him do whatever he wanted with me, I was a flower to be smelled, a fruit to be eaten, I seemed to be sprouting leaves, buds, branches, oh, the changing season! Then he pulled away, pushed down gently on my shoulder and I knelt—my intoxication didn't entirely stop me realizing that he was brutally channel-hopping between two performances: hard actor in an X-rated movie and swooning lover in a romantic soap opera, between Camille and Claire. His heart's in the balance, I thought. But all of it gave me pleasure, I felt at home both here and there, I was auditioning for both parts, I was happy to have it all, with no sharing or compromising, my desire accepted all the contradictions, and with good reason, this man was here, I was taking him, I loved all the different men in him, even the one who felt only contempt for me. He groaned as he let me work on him, gradually releasing his grip on my hair, the exquisite pain of it passed, then he pulled me back up very gently, "You're soft, you're so soft," he said, and held me to him, "I can feel your love," he whispered, and it was true, desire is the moment when love is possible.

We made our way to the bedroom, intertwined, there was a clotheshorse with a woman's clothes drying on it. "I'll leave the light on in the corridor," he said, as he took off all his clothes, "I broke the bedside light." I undressed too, and we lay down and took each other in our arms again.

What I'd like to tell you, Louis, to tell you but not describe, because I'm lazy or I simply can't, because I'm weak or frightened, just tell you, is the strength of that moment. Oh, I don't doubt for a minute that you've experienced it yourself, Louis, I'm not trying to teach you anything, I want to immortalize it—because anything written bears witness. We write in order to have proof, that's all. Books are made up of these memories piling up on each other like leaves becoming soil. Pages of humus. I guess you'll think I'm crazy, but I've often made love so that I could write. Well, I made love to make love, but I've never seen much difference between desire and a desire to write—it's the same vital impulse, the same need to feel the materialness of life. You'll say it's the opposite, that the one compensates for the absence of the other, that we exile ourselves from life in representations of it, that we write because we've stopped fucking—I remember you telling me one time, "literature is for want of flesh"—or that when we write we override our animal instincts, that body and language are not the same thing. That couldn't be further from the truth, and anyway, just remember the other word for language: "tongue," a ridiculous obscenity. I've never been able to use the word "tongue" in its linguistic sense without thinking of the other meaning, without feeling the thing inside my mouth at the same time as the word, without picturing tongues in front of my very eyes, probing for each other, touching and melding together. I need all the depth of language when I write, and its finer qualities too, its softness and its abrasive aspects. I wallow savagely in the French language, I can't imagine doing the same with any other. I lick, and suck, taste and draw things in, I kindle the beginnings of desire with my tongue, and my tongue has its own desire to know. I kiss the dream of a narrative, and kisses always tell me stories. The most beautiful stories are those silently invented by kisses; and anyway we don't actually need words to be loved. Every time I've had writer's block, I've gone out to look for a man, to find life. That's why I saw Chris again, in spite of everything. Not for sex itself, not to orgasm (and did I actually orgasm that first time?) but to feel the strength of desire, to incarnate it, have it in my skin. Because it's not sex I'm interested in, it's desire. The attraction rather than possession. The light-headedness rather than the spasm. My pleasure comes before the moment of ecstasy. I don't aspire to that *petite mort*, to a momentary death, but to the vastness of life, to extreme existence. It's not so much that I desire pleasure as I get pleasure from desire. Love isn't the subject of my books, it's their source. I'm not looking for a story, but the feeling of being alive, and writing that down would ultimately be defeat, and climaxing would be its downfall. Feeling desire for a man is like dreaming a book: everything is wide open, huge and chaotic, there's nothing to stop the galloping horse, and there's fear too, vast vertiginous fear even though we can tell that nothing will make us fall, our power is infinite yet disarmed, oh my, how we run, how hot it is, it's the sun coupled with the wind, reconciled. And the chaos becomes orderly or settles, we know it does even if we do forget this, it becomes a sentence or a blank space, the beginning of something or silence, a story or not. But finding that chaos, that primal force, within words? That will never be achieved. Sitting at a desk, looking at a screen, at a page, the loss is palpable, I can feel eternity withdrawing, low tide. So when there's nothing but sand left, desert as far as the eye can see, I want to find that driving force again, find that pure presence, this absence made up of words is too violent, my flesh needs other flesh to define itself. In the past when I suffered this, when I couldn't write and, because I was alone, I couldn't feel the desire of a physical body, I'd go and scour my bookshelves for something to fill the hole that had been bored open by my fear. I had my own objects of desire, my body of delectation, I knew which page would ease my tension, my urgency, my longing, I often found it straightaway, or I'd rifle through the book shaking in the same way I sometimes do when I'm very hungry, I was hungry for words, I gorged myself on Baudelaire's *Voyage* or La Rochefoucauld's maxims or the end of *Bérénice*. My menu couldn't have been more classic, Louis. But if I really think about it, it wasn't only the French language that sated me. In fact I found even more satisfaction with English or Italian poems, a foreign body was even more satisfying than a familiar one.

> *If you see a fair form, chase it*
> *And if possible embrace it,*
> *Be it a girl or boy.*
> *Don't be bashful; be brash, be fresh.*
> *Life is short, so enjoy*
> *Whatever contact your flesh*
> *May at the moment crave:*
> *There's no sex life in the grave.*

I read out loud, rereading passages ten times, compulsively, the tension dissipated as I read, I was masturbating with words, if you like, and not just words, because I sometimes found I chose Sade. And then I don't know what happened—or rather I know, but this understanding came slowly—either way, a time came when it stopped working, my desire for words evaporated. Dead. Finished. They were no longer enough to soothe me, to fill the void left by a body, by another person. No book had the same effect on me as a living person. It was a very private disaster, the sort you see all the time here, the place where I'm writing now: people who've been killed by separation, who can't be mended with words anymore. We don't want symbols now, we need the real thing. We're fed up with praying, what would really help is an act of grace. "Thank you, Oh Lord, at last I have someone to give me what I so desperately need, to rekindle my lust for life." That's what we want to be saying instead of dwelling on our frustration. Before they brought me here, they found a scrap of paper in my pocket and on it were three sentences that I don't remember writing, but they were in my handwriting: "My kingdom for a horse," and below it, "I'd give all of literature in exchange for love" and "Every word in the world for a mad horse."

Except I was the one they thought was mad.

But I'm getting ahead of myself, I need to finish my story first.

Chris suddenly broke off our lovemaking and masturbated frenetically next to my mouth before— *This is okay, right?*— coming over it. He dropped back onto his side, "Phew, I needed that," he said. Then he jumped to his feet, dressed without even looking at me, and left the room, followed by Daddy. When I joined him he was stabbing at the remote control before eventually settling for a reality show. "Yeah, no, but I'm a princess," some girl was saying, she had lips like a grouper fish and leather hot pants, "It's not easy to get me into bed, I know what I'm worth." I sat down, the audience was clapping, I pretended to watch for a few minutes, but I was hungry and thirsty, I was a bit dazed, my internal parachute hadn't really succeeded in slowing my fall.

"You couldn't uncork the bottle, could you?" I asked.

"Where did you park?" he replied, his eyes still on the screen.

I stood up. "I came by Métro," I said, picking up my purse, "and I'll leave the same way."

"No but you can sleep here if you like, I don't mind, I usually stay watching TV on the sofa, I don't like schedules and constraints, but use the bedroom if you like, it's no problem."

I said no, I'd rather go home, he didn't move. "See ya," I said, pushing Daddy aside with my foot because he was trying to get out, and I slammed the door. He's giving you the Métro treatment all over again, I thought as I headed for the Porte des Lilas. And he didn't even give you the wine you brought yourself! Unbelievable! I didn't understand anything about my humiliation, except that I needed to get the better of it. In the Métro I received a text: "Is everything okay?" Then another two minutes later: "Did you get home all right?" I didn't reply, I would get home, yes, and everything wasn't too bad, actually: I'd come away with the memory of my desire, it was stronger than shame, stronger than anything else. I'd stolen the fire, and paid the price—the lacerating shame in my entrails, like an eagle's beak—but what did that matter? It hurt, yes, but, sitting there in the Métro, I thought it was worth it, it was worth suffering because coming back to life inside me was a longing for words and phrases, pooling together were fragments of sound, a mosaic, an opera, a stream of images, a novel, a film. In my mind I folded the bubble-wrap of memory around his fingers moving toward my breasts, his mouth, the elastic feel of his erect penis in my hand, his fist pulling my hair back as he got into his stride. I wrapped this desire up in my memory to stop it leaking away, or breaking, caution fragile, I wanted to keep hold of it for a while—if you can't write with this, I thought, what *do* you need? The heat was already coming back to me, the desire I'd forgotten like a word on the tip of my tongue, the vital power of it like a seized motor coming to life. Wanting anything from Chris was probably a waste of time, but how is time ever wasted if it results in a book?

He called me the next day, around midday, he was thinking of me, he couldn't wait to see me again, what was I wearing? Right now he was in the corridor, thinking about my mouth, he was jerking off as he remembered it, "and you?" He was thinking about everything we did, but mostly about everything we hadn't yet done, everything we would do, it was going to be so good, "I like everything about you," he said, "your eyes, your mouth, your little breasts, your softness, you're so soft," everything about me turned him on, but most of all my ass, "never seen such a beautiful ass, can I see you this evening?" I said I didn't know. "Don't you want to see me?" he murmured... "Come on, come over. I'm waiting already. Tell me you're coming, say you want to see

me, it's all you can think about." I laughed. "Well, okay…"
"Cool!" he exclaimed happily. "Come at eight o'clock. Do
you remember the code?"

I was in the street when he called back two hours later, I
didn't hear it ring, I was walking with all the majestic power,
the blatant aura of desire, everyone can see it, I made eye
contact with other people and could see they were turned on
or curious, aroused or envious, when you're desired you're
desirable, that's the law, it's the idiot's theorem, but it's easy
to demonstrate, you can read it in people's eyes, the body is
an open book. "Listen, this is such a pain," his message said
in a glum voice, "I'd completely forgotten I'm meant to be
somewhere this evening, I suddenly remembered, so basically, we can catch up tomorrow evening, ciao."

This little game of hide-and-seek went on for several
weeks, we saw each other, we missed each other, he had to
see a friend or his father, it was a merry-go-round of yes and
no, and I played along but it wasn't very merry. Sometimes
when he was just too boorish, I thought of breaking it off,
particularly as the sex itself was disappointing, like a trip
you've dreamed of for ages that turns out to be a letdown.
But my desire had built so many castles in the air that the
ruins were enough for me. Besides, I wasn't really looking
for gratification—I was getting enough pleasure from my
desire. And anyway, with me the desire for love is always
coupled with a desire for familiarity. Curiosity is the sign:
suddenly wanting to know someone, to decipher them.
When the other person becomes a secret. Where there was
simply a body, there's now a story. When a physical form
becomes a bottomless mystery. I was curious and I wasn't

the only one: Claire also wanted to know who Chris was, and which one of us brought out the real him.

One evening he invited me to go see him in Sevran, his parents were away for the whole weekend. I took the high-speed subway, pleased to be seeing him in his usual habitat. He was waiting for me at the station in his Citroën, he proudly talked me through it—"It's gorgeous," I said. My father had one when I was little, I didn't say. After driving for a few minutes we pulled into the parking lot of a housing project. "I warn you, it's very basic." It was a stiflingly clean two-bedroom apartment which felt empty despite the olive green velvet in the living room and the ornaments on the black sideboard. No plants, no books, no magazines, no paintings, except for a small Poulbot cartoon in the hallway and a plate with a fish design hanging on the kitchen wall: it was like a show home—showing what exactly? What deficiencies, what anxieties, what fears about life? What crime against happiness? Chris's room had more life to it, but it was a past life: soccer club flags, model cars, photos of school picnics, a Guns N' Roses poster, a baseball cap. "So this is my place," he said, taking me in his arms. I huddled close to him, touched. "Will you take me out to a restaurant?" he asked, pushing me away.

It was a strange dinner, us hovering between mute old couple and cute e-couple. That must be Chris's problem, I thought—maybe it was everyone's problem? What role to give sex in a relationship? No role at all? Or center stage? When he looked at me I could feel myself switching constantly between sex bomb and old friend. You see, Louis, if I'd decided to write a novel about this sorry affair, I'd have described every aspect of our sexuality, I'd have literally written a sex report. I know lots of people don't like that, particularly men, if it's a woman writer, maybe you most of all, you think it's vulgar, or you think we should leave it to men, it's their field. Well, I'm fascinated by sexuality. In life. And therefore in books. I don't know anything about a man till I've slept with him. Nothing important. Nothing real. At best, whatever I've glimpsed by talking to him and spending time with him can be confirmed by sex. But it's often contradicted instead. The whole social construct dissolves when two bodies come together or, if the construct stays standing, then that's because it's all there is: an obsession with control, with fear or negation of the other person, a longing for power. Otherwise, sex is the truest and most fragile form of sharing, when desire and tenderness make us generous, when the present moment looks deceptively like love, and we often are deceived, we surrender to the fire, we throw ourselves in without realizing it will burn, like innocents, but it's a beautiful deception, this deception is far from deceitful, we are innocent in our desire and that's what we're hoping for, to be literally innocent, for there to be nothing noxious about us, nothing harmful, to do no harm, in fact, to want only the best, to receive only the best, an exchange of breath and tongues, of something real and real words. To describe sex is to illustrate humanity, its potential goodness, its transfiguring power as well as its shared weakness, an acceptance of a common fate that acts as a backdrop to life. Otherwise it shows hate, domination, and shame. Either way, sex is familiarity, instant knowledge, it may well be volatile, it may lead to oblivion, but surely then it's up to literature to catch it on the wing?

After dinner we went back to his childhood bedroom. We didn't make love, he came too quickly and turned to face the wall straightaway. In the night he howled like an eviscerated animal and held me so tightly I couldn't breathe. "Oh Camille," he cried, "oh Camille, my Camille," then he went back to sleep with an agonized sob, not relaxing his grip. I was suffocating, I extricated myself as best I could, disturbed by his behavior, and I shivered with cold the rest of the night because he'd wound himself up in the duvet like a swaddled baby. In the morning he put a spoonful of honey in my tea, which he handed to me like a precious gift. There was nothing to eat, not even a crust of bread. I think it was then, amid my brutally disappointed desire, in that moment of nocturnal weakness when my name—Camille, not Claire—intruded, that the story of Chris and me, in all its arid inadequacy, started to be written in my mind.

We continued seeing each other like that, at my place or his cousin's, in rocky but increasing intimacy. Each of us had shown something of ourselves to the other: his desire, his fear—which was hesitantly abating. He was less afraid of being misjudged and scorned, I was less frightened of not being loved—what is love exactly? What is it if not a longing to be repeatedly reunited with the same body, and the narrative we've constructed about it? But the question of money still hung in the air. He never had any, he borrowed Métro tickets from me, ten euros to buy cigarettes, a hundred to fill the car with gas, never gave me the change, suggested the gifts I could bring back for him from my trips—the latest Nikes from New York or some piece of junk from Cambrai. I think he even scooped up the tips I left for waiters at café tables, or those other people left. He criticized the way my apartment was decorated, wanted me to replace all the paintings with photos he'd taken, which I could buy at "buddy's rates."

Every time we saw each other he told me how fed up he was with Sevran and his view over concrete, he took beautiful pictures of the suburbs, the corridors in their high-speed subway stations, the residential skyscrapers, the gray faces. But what he wanted was the sky, the sea, wide open space, snapping blue and wind and expanse. And I wanted to give him what he wanted; and also another taste of the life you can have at home with a man—since Joe, I hadn't had that sweet feeling of a confined space, and the relationship that develops between that intimate space and the space in which your body relaxes surrounded by the smell of coffee, of old lofts and fireplaces. So I decided to rent a house at Cap Blanc-Nez. It was wild and beautiful, out of season, we'd be fine there. I liked how happy he was when I told him—a child who's never seen the sea.

His Citroën broke down three days before we left—"Not cool," he said on the phone. It was in a garage in Sevran, it was the carburetor, it was likely to cost several hundred euros. Not to mention the lens that was stolen from his bag during a shoot and that he'd have to replace. He couldn't see how to cope, and our vacation would have to fall through, unless I could lend...I told him I'd rent a car, the house was already paid for, we weren't going to give up. I didn't have too much money myself, my advance had been eaten up long since, Louis, my not very stupendous advance, Louis, but I so wanted a vacation and to be with him. The next day Chris called me when I was about to go to my local car rental. He would take care of renting something in Sevran, his father was lending him the money to fix his car. He'd come over with the rental car that same evening, and we'd set off the next morning. I said okay—cars are a man thing. He texted me to ask if I could transfer the rental money into his account, which I did right away.

That evening he parked on the street outside my apartment and called out to me from the sidewalk, "My beloved! I forgot the code." I went down to open the door, he took me in his arms and danced me around: "You're my little woman! You're my little fairy." It was a tender night, wrapped snugly around us. In the morning we stuffed all our bags in the trunk and set off excitedly, hoist 'em high, sailor. He drove the whole way and I slept. I woke to hear the radio blaring at the top of its lungs, "Can't Buy Me Love," a Beatles song from 1964. "Never heard that song before," Chris said, "have you? It's cool."

"I have, yes, vaguely," I said, stretching. "But I was only a little girl in '64."

The car—a red Citroën DS Special Series, an overequipped descendant of his vintage model—swerved and ground violently to a halt in a deserted rest area. We can't have been far from the sea, the air coming through the open window smelled of salt. Chris turned to me, both hands clamped on the wheel, his jaw set like iron.

"What's the—?" I said.

He scowled at me harshly. "You're over fifty?" He pinched his lips together and asked again, louder: "You're over fifty?" I looked at him but didn't answer. "Well, that really flips me out," he said, and he climbed out and slammed the door savagely.

"I'm the same age I was last night," I wailed through the windshield.

In the supermarket where we stopped to buy provisions, he walked along the aisles ten feet ahead of me, not turning around once, letting me push the shopping cart like the more-than-fifty-year-old housewife I'd become in the space of a three-minute single. He just tossed a jack for an mp3 player into the cart. "Do you like tomatoes?" I asked, suppressing my humiliation once again. "What shall we eat this evening?"

"You're the one shopping," he replied contemptuously. Then, because I kept asking, he said, "I've never seen anyone less like a woman." Even my housewife status had evaporated. He joked with the girl at the checkout while I put the credit card in the machine. She had a tattoo of a crocodile on her wrist, he smiled and showed her his, birds with their wings spread open, "You're going to gobble me up," he said. Then he walked out without helping me carry the bags. In the parking lot he opened the trunk and watched me put the bags in.

"Thank you," I said.

In Boulogne I went to pick up the keys to the house from the owners, he didn't come in with me, and when the couple saw me to the door, he barely acknowledged them, as if he were just a paid driver, waiting, leaning on the hood in the sunshine. A subtle smell of decomposition wafted up from the embankment. "Okay, I'll drive now," I said, walking around the back of the car, "I'd like to see what's so special about this DS."

He snapped his hand toward the ignition and took out the key. I raised my eyebrows. "No way are you driving," he said, crossing his arms; a blood vessel bulged in his neck.

"And why not?" Tears were gathering at the back of my eyes, probably the light. "Because I don't let anyone drive my car, that's all."

I laughed. "Your car? YOUR car? May I remind you that *I* paid for this car? And I like driving too."

"Maybe you do, but you won't be driving now. Anyway, it wouldn't be legal, you're not a designated driver."

"Great! Well, that's not a problem, I'll call the agency and ask them to add me. Pass me the receipt. That was a bit much! Did you really think I'd spend two weeks here without driving? And be completely dependent on you? And your moods?" I took out my cell phone, he didn't move, just stared off into the distance, as if he couldn't hear me. "Do you have their number? Hand me the receipt..."

"I won't give you the receipt, and you won't be calling the agency."

"Oh really? And why not?" My voice was strangulated, as if I had a hand to my throat.

"Because I don't want my name to be associated with yours."

"It's just so I can drive, you know, it's not to publish the banns of marriage."

"We're not together," he roared. "Do you get that? We. Are. Not. Together! I don't love you and I'm not with you. Get it?"

What a dick, I thought. "Yes we are. Look, we're both here, together," I said mischievously, and in that moment I lightly swiped the keys from his hand and started to run. He followed me around the car and I laughed. "We're no longer together but you're still chasing me," I crowed between peals of laughter, I still wanted to believe we could get out of the situation like that, by laughing about the lack of love, or I wanted to give the owners of the house their money's worth, they could have been watching through their white lace curtains. I ran down the street so they could no longer see me, Chris caught up with me, I'd miscalculated his lack of humor, he rammed me against a wall, grabbed my wrist with one hand and with the other tried to prize open my fingers that were holding the keys. I was still laughing but he was hurting me, on a level with my eyes I could see his biceps swelling dangerously, dangerously, I thought. Danger, I thought

"Camille, give me back the keys now." I struggled a little to show my strength, because I'm strong too, I was strong, I wanted him to see that, I clutched those keys in my fist, they dug into my palm, my back burrowed into the wall as if it wanted to disappear into it. Chris kept up the pressure, my fingers were giving in to his, "You're hurting me," I said, "stop." I flailed my arms to escape his clutches, he caught me by the wrist again, raised my hand high and immobilized me by holding it tight like a referee in the boxing ring, and with that gesture which announced me as the winner he won. I let go of the keys for fear of hearing my own bones break. He went back to the car, and so did I, he walked like John Wayne, we climbed in without another word and drove to the house, with me telling him the way in a GPS voice.

It was a beautiful traditional stone house, spacious and cold. There were three bedrooms, one of which contained a child's bed and another an old-fashioned cradle beside a double bed—I had something similar for my dolls back in the day. I rearranged the drapes just as I used to then, saw myself as a child. I put the sheets and pillowcases into the largest bedroom and put the food into the fridge. My wrist hurt and the index finger on that hand was red and swollen, I had at least two dislocated fingers. Chris was building a fire in the grate, I could hear him moving logs. The evening wind was up outside, it slipped under the doors with a keening sound like an injured dog, and the trees waved wildly in the gathering gloom. "I don't think this is going to work," I said, going over to him, "we can't do this."

"Okay," Chris replied, pushing the kindling around to put out the fire just as it was taking, "let's go." He jumped to his feet and the bulk of him frightened me.

I backed away and said, "Not tonight, look, it's already dark and there's a storm on the way, it would be dangerous. Let's stay the night here and we'll see if it's calmed down in the morning." I meant the weather and us. The fire had reddened his cheeks, he had the flushed face of a lover.

"Okay," he said quickly, "okay." He fanned the embers, then sat on the couch, facing me. I opened my laptop and he his, the Internet connection wasn't very good, he put his earphones in and started clicking his fingers in time to music I couldn't hear. After a while he stood up, rummaged in a cupboard, and flicked on the kettle. With a questioning gesture, he offered me a coffee, I shook my head, no. He made himself a sandwich, looking furious, then came around behind me to check the fire. "What are you looking at?" he asked.

"Nothing." I quickly closed my laptop. I'd been onto the Avis Web site to see if I could add myself as a second driver, but I didn't want him to know. Once in my life I'd been physically afraid of a man, my husband in a fit of jealousy, wild-eyed, he'd slapped me with all his might, I ended up with a detached retina, but I was young and I thought it was the price a girl had to pay for being desirable, that it made men mad, that it was natural. I had to have laser treatment.

Now it was the other way around: I'd become undesirable and the man couldn't bear it, he felt belittled. It wasn't natural, it was social—his image of himself in the world: a Brahman among the untouchables, I thought. Untouchable, I thought. *Over fifty!* Even though we were alone he was consumed with shame, his mouth pinched by it, he'd been betrayed, he'd been humiliated, I was there in front of him like a mirror, a visual display of his decline. The white drapes on the cradle glowed in the shadows, and I tried to understand: was it being with a woman who could no longer have children that suddenly appalled him? Some sort of mix-up men might make between infertility and impotence?

A loathing of sterility? A subconscious fear of sleeping with their own mother? A fear that—conversely—young women wouldn't have about sleeping with their fathers? They might even be looking for them. And the fathers too? Not afraid of sleeping with the daughters? But why? Why this asymmetry that was so universally accepted and validated? Why this superior caste for men?

Basically, Louis, I was trying to behave as I usually do when disaster threatens: I drew on the power of reason, I countered my fear with ideas, I thought in order to ease the suffering, I used intelligence to bandage my wounds.

But the system had its failings this time, I could tell. Intelligence wasn't enough to ensure my safety, it made me see the truth in too harsh a light. Being put right is worse than being treated wrong, you're no longer protected by any illusions, you're left with nothing over your eyes to conceal the truth—no veil to cover its dazzling nakedness. The truth is what never changes, the thing we can't influence. And realizing that is terrifying. So you have to drive the thought out and rally your whole body in your skin, reignite feelings of pleasure, try to compensate for unhappiness with life.

"Look, there are some CDs…What sort of music do you like?" I put on a Manu Chao album and started dancing wildly, the chirpy rhythm leading me into oblivion, completely emptying my head. Chris might come and dance with me, I thought. Dancing is like sex—a way of getting closer without resorting to words. But he got up, exasperated, gathered his things, and went and shut himself in the back bedroom. The storm raged, branches smacked against the windows, the lights flickered, and I clung to the wind as I danced.

"I warn you, I'm leaving at eight p.m." This curt sentence, lobbed from the bedroom doorway, stirred me from heavy sleep. Eight p.m., I thought, that gives us plenty of time for a reconciliation. The clock said 7:30—a.m. With another man, and if I'd had a better night behind me, I'd have said, "Come here, please, come to bed, let's make love, come on, then we'll see about later"—that's what Circe suggests to the furious Ulysses, because the flesh can soften the mood—it's the only thing to do, make love. But pasty-mouthed and puffy-eyed, I didn't say anything, I gave a vague groan and buried myself under the duvet.

Now I open my eyes and it's 8:20, the house is filled with silence, the wind has dropped. I get up, a baleful glance at the scary mirror in the bathroom, a double layer of concealer under my eyes, a dusting of blusher, putting on makeup, pleasing, pleasing, pleasing, getting back to desire. I listen to the silence. Chris's door is closed. It's cold in the big living room, even the embers look frozen.

I switch on the kettle at the breakfast bar, put two slices of bread in the toaster, pick up an empty packet of Camels. The front door is ajar. I walk onto the doorstep barefoot, the car's no longer parked outside, he's gone to the village for cigarettes, I throw away the Camel packet, the sky's blue-gray, I turn on the radio, *Oh you'll see, you'll see, that's what love's all about.* The coffee percolates as slowly as the time. I knock on his bedroom door, open it, the room's empty, his things have gone, all that's left are the dirty utensils and the leftovers of his dinner on the bedside table. I'll have to clean up, that's what he wants when it comes down to it, for me to stick to my woman's role. There's a Tintin book on the bed among the rumpled covers. He's on voicemail. I instinctively call Avis in Sevran and, shivering with cold, ask whether I could possibly change the rental contract. "Oh, but the gentleman has just called…I've already explained it all to him, he said he'd bring the car back at around three o'clock." "Three o'clock…and what about the refund?" "We'll give you a pro-rata refund to match your usage. So you hired it for ten days at two hundred fifty euros, you're bringing it back today, we'll count that as two days, we'll reimburse the difference. If the car's in good condition, of course." "Why did you say two hundred fifty euros?" "That's what you paid, madam." "No, no, we paid three hundred thirty. Was there extra insurance?" The woman's voice is less confident. "Um, listen, I have the invoice in front of me, there's an all-inclusive offer this month for Citroën DSs, your husband, well, the gentleman paid two hundred fifty euros."

I tell her everything, spill out the whole story. She's a stranger, but she's a woman. She says "Oh yes" and "that's terrible" and "I understand," and this is all that matters right now: to have a woman understand, and agree with me that it's terrible.

"You've got through to Chris's voicemail. I'm not here but leave me a message and I'll call you back, and that's a promise." And that's a promise. That was the last time I heard his voice—a pretty stupid voice, to be honest, I thought. My shame was more painful than the abandonment, because I had only myself to blame. He'd already blocked me on Facebook—I couldn't even leave a private message, a bandaged thumb icon made the grim statement: "This link is no longer available."

And that's a promise.

The idea of resuscitating Claire Antunes didn't come to me immediately. Don't say I'm cynical, Louis, nothing was premeditated. My anger and contempt kept me going for an hour or two. Then loneliness moved in and the sense of abandonment nestled in the little cradle, I couldn't take my eyes off it, it was empty and there I was lying in it, it was me there howling to the point of suffocation. When the stress became too much, I tried to get help from women who could explain or at least understand—women who knew Chris, up close or distantly. On Facebook I sent a private message to Charlotte, an ex he'd sometimes mentioned; to the actress we'd met together at the café that first evening; to two other girls who often liked his posts and whose names I remembered.

To each of them I briefly described what had happened, I wasn't asking for anything specific, just a bit of sisterly support, that was all, without having to draw them a picture. It was the first time I'd expected more of a woman than a man—the first time in my life since childhood, since my mother. Why strangers rather than friends? I don't know. Perhaps the shame didn't weigh so heavily with them. Two of them answered kindly, two blocked me—this link is no longer available. Alix, the actress, gave me her number; I called her.

She wasn't surprised, she knew his type, good-looking, narcissistic, and shallow, self-interested and weak, oh, my word, did she know them, she collected them even. She said I shouldn't leave, after all it was my vacation too, I could enjoy the fresh air, the ocean, the free time, the house miles from Paris, I was lucky; she meanwhile was waiting tables to pay for her acting classes.

I couldn't leave anyway. The wind and rain had started again, the storm moaned at the windows. And where would I go? How? Because we were driving I hadn't thought twice about bringing three bags filled with sheets, books, rain boots and walking boots. A parody of the bourgeois seaside vacationer, that's what I was. With all that weighing me down, I couldn't even reach the bus stop on foot, and that's if there was one within five miles. The house was isolated, it was off season, almost all the shutters in the village were closed. I was alone.

I stayed there, prostrate, all day, slumped on the sofa drinking tea. In my mind's eye, I followed the car's progress back to Paris. My thoughts now operated only like a forsaken GPS, all roads led away from me, all paths went nowhere. Then I played Manu Chao on a loop and danced till I was exhausted. I danced and my memory dismissed the past and all its attendant emotions. Now I had no parents or children, no house or home, I was godless and lawless. I was abandoned, in a state of abandon, banned from everything under the drapes of that cradle, the shroud of a tomb. I said things out loud, disconnected words that clattered like cannonballs chained to a convict's ankles.

It was only the next day that, with no news of any sort, I thought of resuming the conversation in Claire Antunes's identity. She alone could now pick up the baton, taking over from me, taking over all of me, I would fade away, melt away, I could feel myself becoming no one and I liked it, I was turning into nothing and it suited me fine, but the pleasure I took in my own annihilation brought me up short, I needed to do something, anything to reestablish a connection, even if it was through the other woman in me. So I sent Chris a message from Claire's Facebook: "Hi Chris, how are you after all this time? I'm still in Lisbon. But hey, I received a weird message on messenger, I'm forwarding it to you, it upset me, did you really do that? I can't believe you did. Claire." I attached the message I'd sent to some of his girlfriends.

He replied immediately: "You're right not to believe it, Claire. That woman's completely crazy, she's telling lies all over the place to get to me, but my friends just laugh because they know me, they know I couldn't dream up all that garbage, you should block her right away otherwise she'll poison your life. Real sorry to be back in touch with you because of that head case, but at least she did that for us. Let's hear some of your news. How are you, *bonita*? Are you coming back to France? *Beijos*. PS did you notice, I've taken up Portuguese while I'm waiting for you."

I persisted: "But were you at the seaside together? Is that true? I know who she is, I read two of her books, I really like her work, she's a great writer" (oh yes, Louis, I wrote those words).

Him: "We're NOT together. We went away to that house to work on a photo book project, she said she wanted to do a book with me but she was actually in love with me, it was an excuse to lure me to that house, but I got the picture, I'm not an idiot. When I saw what was going on, you can imagine I took my car and left, and that's it. Does being a writer impress you, then? Not me, I like real people. And I can tell you she's super nasty in real life, she told me some horrible stuff, she was completely hysterical and that's something I can't take, and so you see now she's trying to bring me down with my friends. But forget about it, who gives a damn about her. Tell me about you, how are things? Are you happy? Do you still think about me?"

Claire: "I'm okay. Sorry to go on about this, Chris, but I'm worried she'll be in really bad shape, all alone in that house. You say she's nasty but if I put myself in her shoes and if someone did that to me, I'd go crazy. You abandoned her there? And she says it was a car she rented, not your car. That you were together. And that you twisted her arm, that she's going to file a complaint with the police. None of that's true?"

Chris: "Like I said, she's crazy. Fuck it, this is ridiculous! Are you messaging her or something? You'll have to choose, huh?! When I say it's my car, that means it's my car, okay? I'm just telling the truth, okay? Now do what you like, Claire, but I'm real disappointed, this is so not cool, I expected better of you."

I didn't reply. I built a fire in the hearth as best I could, and let the flames tell me my fate, they're very good at that, they hypnotize heartache. The bruise on my arm was going a fiery color, it looked like a Turner. My body softened in the heat like wax melting.

He was the one to get back in touch with me, well, with Claire, the next day. "Okay, Claire, I'm sorry about yesterday, but you have to understand, I won't tolerate lies. I don't have it in me to hurt a woman, for God's sake! What else did she tell you? I need to be careful, her slander could damage my reputation, she's really nasty, like I said, she can spread her garbage on Facebook and on other sites."

Claire: "She's stopped messaging me, but her last message was worrying. She's all alone in that house, it must be scary, are you sure she's okay?"

Chris: "Yeah, she's just acting up, she's lying to get your sympathy. She's actually back in Paris, a buddy went over to see her, she's fine but psychologically she's in bad shape. Apparently there's only one thing she wants, and that's for me to call. She can wait as long as she likes. None of this is my fault, she just needs to forget me, I already forgot her" (winky face emoticon).

With each new message from Claire, I hoped he'd snap, and if he didn't actually admit the truth to her, at least call me, the real me, to apologize, explain, and see how I was, if I needed anything. I couldn't bring myself to believe that the profoundly human emotion experienced in romantic desire had so completely disappeared and been replaced by such total denial, and yet with each new message I was confronted with the same irrefutable fact: the link was no longer available.

You'll say I had it coming, Louis, and—at the end of the day—my punishment wasn't that bad, although cruel. Just revisiting a frivolous eighteenth-century novel, nothing more. Contemporary *Dangerous Liaisons*, with me as both Merteuil and Tourvel, manipulator and victim, the one who dies and the one who kills. I'd toyed with fiction, and it had just come boomeranging back like a surprise twist at the end of a novel. KissChris had regained the upper hand, refusing to be my plaything. Good for him! Even I, in the brief moments of respite I had from my lethargy, could imagine the ironic account I would give of events once I was feeling better. Despite my increasing physical weakness, or perhaps because of it, I still hadn't gauged the ravages that this abandonment—which Claire still wanted to call just rude behavior—was currently effecting.

At first I found things to do. I explored the house, opened closets, tried on men's clothes and women's. I spent one night in the children's bedroom, at the foot of the cradle. I ran away by dispersing myself about the place. I sought refuge in books. There was a remarkable collection, I remember, a peculiar mixture of holiday reading—beach books, Michelin Guides, sailing manuals—and rare or confidential works, limited editions on velum, precious sonnets, little-known contemporary authors. I read everything I could lay my hands on, using words to fill the gap left by silence, but apart from a few poems, it didn't work very well. There was also one of those phony psychology manuals, a thing with forms and tests for identifying difficult personalities, and a book about the signs of the Zodiac. Chris was paranoid, narcissistic, passive-aggressive, obsessive around the edges with schizoid tendencies. I was Scorpio with Libra rising, with the sensitivity of Cancer, the perseverance of Capricorn, and the generosity of Leo. At least, that was how I saw myself in the comic description I would give of my misadventure, trying in vain to stimulate my urge to write.

There was even a point when I softened toward Chris: I remembered the last thing he'd said to me, "I'm leaving at eight p.m.," obviously he meant to say eight a.m., but some small part of him—his duty to be a man, to incarnate the law?—had driven him to this slip of the tongue, in which I detected his distress, like a child yelling insults to stop himself from crying. But it was too slight a detail to bring me back to life. Over the next few days everything slowed down. I now got up only to make tea, take a piss, or take another book from the shelves—not that I was reading them anymore. The only one I now remember is this, because it was the last status I posted on my wall—a collection by Claude Esteban:

> *I have days*
> *I no longer need, I give*
> *Them to you, they might*
> *Grow in someone else's care, become light,*
> *Silky, full of sunshine,*
> *Whereas I put them in a gray*
> *Box underground*
> *And see them rot, take them from me,*
> *Make them live,*
> *Let them become children who play*

The rest is a blur, I can still picture the sun coming back through the bay window, a big pebble resting on the corner of the coffee table, the tartan blanket wrapped around me, the dwindling daylight. The kettle plugged in on the bar in the American-style kitchen was now out of reach, the stereo too. I just remember sleeping with my eyes open, I'm sure of that. And telling myself that nightfall was really the day falling away, a moment identified by language as two contradictory formulations that meant the same thing. I remember savoring that discovery as the last pleasure offered to me by language.

When the owners arrived on the day we were meant to hand back the keys, they found me half unconscious, soaked in sweat and urine. They called the police and an ambulance, because my arm was covered with bruises and they thought I'd been attacked. While they waited for the emergency services to arrive they asked me questions, I answered with a flood of ranting words while flattening my breasts with my hands as if trying to iron them: that's what they told me later, in the hospital, where they came to see me. Very kind. I'd lost eleven pounds, my hair was falling out, I was delirious, but not so much that I forgot to say they mustn't contact my daughters, or anyone. I didn't tell the police anything, didn't even mention that Chris had been there, at least I don't think I did: apparently I was rambling. After a few days they transferred me to La Forche, and I'm still here, that's where I'm writing from. But don't worry, I'm fine, now, absolutely fine.

Do you know La Forche? It's a psychiatric clinic, there are lots of depressives here—quite a few teachers, some suicidals, mostly women, not that men don't attempt suicide, of course they do, but they hit their target, men go the whole hog with everything. At first I didn't understand why I was here, I wasn't depressed, I was repressed: the vital energy had been knocked out of me, that was all. In fact I slept for days and wept for weeks, but there had been an eclipse of time, to the extent that the thread of time had snapped. If my girls had been there, if I'd had to see them soon, I'd have held it together. But they were far away, they had no idea what was going on, so I could dissolve without causing any harm, I could stop trying to fool anyone, be myself, in other words: nothing. My diagnosis was simple, I didn't need a doctor for that, I could do that all by myself: I didn't have a single cent of desire left, not a kopek, nada. I was a gambler who'd wagered down to the shirt on her back and lost, I was naked, no one to wrap even a sheet around me, to take my hand, never gamble your whole heart, I'd placed my bet out of overweening confidence, no, out of humility, despair, no I'd bet out of excessive pride, I'd risked it all on an uneven bet and out of loss because I'd already lost everything, I could afford to lose because it was all gone already I'd lost big-time lost in a lostissimo sort of way I thought I was queen of the lost I thought I could do this, me, queen of desire, I could become trash, could tolerate denial annihilation brutal irremediable loss bankruptcy failure suicidal downfall, I thought I could always be reborn from the ashes, rise again from the dust that I'd so thoroughly bitten, I wouldn't die suffocated by the earth they shoveled over me. My desire was the seat of my resistance, my internal blockhouse, shelter for my body and my language, I thought it was unassailable, infallible, indestructible. I desire therefore I live, my stainless steel motto. And suddenly there I was, surrounded by my own likeness — oh yes, and like it or not, they were like me, lost, losers — there I was, disarmed, dropped like a stone at the bottom of a well. I couldn't move anymore, didn't want to. It wasn't my pride that had suffered, it was my vital energy. I'd stopped persevering with the idea of living, with the idea I'd always had of what it meant to live. "Strange to have stopped desiring desires," I whispered to myself. All around me I saw my twin shadows wandering around their insubstantial death with a gentle smile or a bitter sneer. We'd all reached the horizon, all understood that beyond the optical horizon was not a line but a single point, period, the end. "That's what everyone's looking for," I thought, "the greatest possible sorrow so that we can each become ourselves before we die." It was a peaceful sort of knowledge, but that may have been the drugs.

Maybe you think I'm taking this too far, Louis, like my mother. That the "greatest possible sorrow" can't be some guy stealing a few hundred euros and dumping you. That there are infinitely worse things: a bereavement, an illness, even divorce is more painful. You're right, on the surface. In actual fact, the same thing has happened to everyone in this place—the depressed, the anxious, the addicts, the anorexics: we've all lost. Something or someone. A love, a fight, an illusion. Or just a meaning—a direction, a significance.

I talked to an analyst here, of course. His name's Marc, but I can change that. He's very good-looking. He insisted on trying to explain that desire and love aren't the same thing. Desire wants to conquer and love wants to keep hold, he says. According to him, desire means having something to win, and love something to lose. But I don't see any difference, all desire is love, because at the time when I want the object of my desire, when I strain toward it, I know that I'll lose it, that I'm already losing it by pursuing it. My desire is both vital power and crazy melancholy — crazy enough to tie up, crazy enough to lock away. I feel as if I've always been like this, that in a way it's a terrifying strength: I can't lose anything, I can't lose, because everything's already lost. So I can confront anything, there are no risks because there's nothing at stake, because I have nothing to lose.

But back there at Cap Blanc-Nez, I had violent proof of my own presumptuousness: I certainly did have something to lose, and the loss of it was life-threatening. I'd lost a sense of loss, I was lacking in lack and I wasn't even trying to find it anymore. With his contempt, Chris had excluded me from the circle, he'd made me ashamed to be alive. Exiled, driven out of the garden of delights. No man left to touch me, no book left to write. I'm talking about desire, Louis. I'd never been afraid of it before, or ashamed, I was its equal. Desire makes us aware of the void, that much is true, of the powerful chaos all around us and within us, but we're aware of that void the way a tightrope walker is aware of the rope, feeling our way like an acrobat reaching his leg forward onto it, we're a hair's breadth from disaster and falling, from mortal terror, and yet there we are, all aquiver with inflated presence, ten times our usual selves, huge, moving through the chaos, held by the single thread of whatever connects us to the other person, our companion in the void, our twin tightrope walker. When are we ever more alive? Happier? Freer? I'm talking about desire, about the impatient slowness of desire. The act itself is different, we're already on our way back to the world, in a position of control, of know-how, it's the same with a book, with what we publish, what we make public, that's what's left of the vast chaos that was a desire for this particular book, the plans for it, the dream of it. A book doesn't keep all the promises of that desire, it is one of its end results. But it translates the pleasure that came after the surge of desire, its epiphany. If a book doesn't have that, it doesn't have anything. The sexual act is the same: the anxiety of desire abates, the hunger, the voracity is calmed, but what desire wants—making love—doesn't gratify it, not completely, there's something left, a lack, and it's on that lack that desire builds again. René Char says that a poem is "the love realized by desire that has stayed as desire." I think that's what a book should be, in an ideal world, and also a meeting: something took place, the desire was there, its searing presence, love happened, sometimes it's perfect, the book is beautiful, vibrant, alive—and yet nothing is possessed, there's nothing to hold in your hand, in your arms, and desire sets its aim at the next moment, already straining in the waiting process, in the acute scalding languor, the chaotic but structured, total but fragmented languor that identifies it, hovering above a fear of the void. "No one possesses nothing... Perhaps our fundamental exercise constitutes loving and writing empty-handed."

There are lots of suicide attempts here. Lots of people who suddenly lost it, at home, at work, or wherever, following what others often see as a minor incident—a cigarette turned down, a disappointing memo, a taunt. Heckled teachers. Broken hearts, too, of course. Inconsolable break-ups. People who can no longer even find a word for what they've lost—can't find the right word—without resorting to images and silence. After a few weeks, it didn't take long, Marc suggested I run a writing workshop for the residents, he thought it would help everyone: them to symbolize their pain, as he put it; me to reconnect with the urge to write, to become a writer again. Because I couldn't write a single line, it was just as impossible as asking an injured bird to fly, I'd had my wings clipped. I agreed.

There are mostly women in my workshop. That's how I met Claire, "clear as Claire can be," she says when she introduces herself. Her husband abandoned her and went off with her younger sister or her niece, I've forgotten. She couldn't take it, lost her self-confidence. She leaves, then comes back. She stays here. Her anger will save her, I think. Or her laughter. There's also Josette, she was raped. And Catherine, she's sixteen, her boyfriend posted pictures of her naked on Facebook, she was hounded on the Net, she threw herself off a bridge. Then there's Michel, who spends his time studying etymology, mostly Hebrew, the meaning of words, their origins. Apparently when he was little he was adopted, and his birth mother was identified only as X, but then his adopted parents sent him back to the orphanage. He never says anything except to tell us the meaning of a word. He doesn't go anywhere without his dictionary—"which has *x*'s all the way through it," as Marc said the other day, it was a good point. He comes to the workshop too. Each of them tells his or her story, or some-one else's, or the one they're dreaming of.

In the early days I was dead. Impossible to write even a sentence, the words sounded like something falling to the floor. I helped the others get started, encouraging them to reinvent life through language, but I couldn't do it myself. I was emptied, empty, old. I couldn't find help anywhere. It went on quite a long time, Louis, so you can see why I didn't give you much news. And then two things happened. First, we decided to put on a play. It was Claire's idea, in a former life she was a renowned specialist in Marivaux and the eighteenth century. We made up our minds to put on *Les fausses confidences*, do you know it? Almost everyone in the group got involved, except the most depressed. And it was in that work on the voice, in gestures and those bodies moving about the stage that a flicker of a flame came back to life. Not just in me, I know that, even though any kind of fire is always precarious here.

The second thing was Christian showing up—Chris to his nearest and dearest, he said. He's a video maker, he was doing a documentary about La Forche. A serious project, fully immersive. He came to the workshop regularly, not as a documentary maker, but as a participant. He never asked to film those sessions, he wanted to be part of the group. One day he admitted that he'd had depression a few years earlier, because a woman with whom he'd had the beginnings of a relationship had committed suicide. That day he wrote a really beautiful text, it was called "The First Time," I've kept it, I often reread it. He explained that he could make love to a woman only once, that he put all of himself into it, all his tenderness, his virility. And afterward he couldn't do it again, it became impossible, physically impossible. He didn't know why. So he'd run away, or become sufficiently obnoxious for the woman to leave him before realizing his failing. Women didn't understand, that first night had been so intense. He'd pulled the wool over people's eyes for a long time by constantly changing partners, until this woman's suicide. And then he was lost, only his work kept him going, he wanted to do well.

To celebrate the end of filming, which went on for weeks, he gave a little party at La Forche. I hadn't danced for an eternity—since Cap Blanc-Nez. When Chris came to ask me to dance, I thought I wouldn't know how to put one foot in front of the other, even for a slow song, but I was actually afraid I would have forgotten how to touch a man's body. Claire was dancing with Marc, *take me now baby here as I am, hold me close, try and understand.* Catherine was spinning slowly by herself, singing under her breath, *desire is hunger is the fire I breathe, love is a banquet on which we feed.* Josette was DJing, *come on now try and understand the way I feel when I'm in your hands, Take my hand come undercover, They can't hurt you now can't hurt you now.* There was a smell of vetiver hanging in the air, the fragrance my father used to wear, I smelled it when he twirled me in his arms, Chris didn't talk at all, I could feel his heart beating, *Because the night belongs to lovers, Because the night belongs to lust, Because the night belongs to lovers, Because the night belongs to us.* Then Michel walked through those of us who were dancing saying that what was always translated in Ecclesiastes as "vanity," "vanity of vanities," *hevel havalim,* specifically meant the condensation from our mouths in winter. Thank you, Michel, I said. At the end of the dance I went outside with Chris and he lit a cigarette. The air was freezing, a few snowflakes fell on the daffodils by the bench. "Vanity of vanities," Chris cried, and we laughed at the condensation. It was very cold, but we were alive in the cold. Chris did it again, shouting at the top of his lungs, "Vanity of vanities," I did too, and then we laughed, oh my how we laughed, we laughed like crazy.

epilogue

Listen, Mr. Deligne, I did what you asked. You're my attorney, I'm paying you enough as it is so I shouldn't have to do the work for you. You wanted concrete proof that my wife has no intention of coming back to real life and doesn't want to take care of our children, and I've given it to you on a platter. What's the problem? I just don't see.

Yes, but that's only because the family law judge is a woman! Is there really no way we can ask for a different judge? I'm sure a man would understand better.

Of course I won't say that in front of her! Do you think I'm an idiot? I just think her obstinacy is unfair and misplaced. After all, I did nothing wrong.

But what difference does it make that Katia's my wife's niece? She's not *my* niece. And I love her. And she loves me. Can't you marry the person you love anymore in this country?

By marriage, Mr. Deligne, by *marriage*, remember that! I'm her uncle by *marriage*. No blood relationship. And let's be sensible about this: if, as I've been asking for months, I finally get this divorce, Katia will no longer have any connection to me, either biologically or "by marriage," and I'll be free to marry her. It's pretty straightforward. Even a four-year-old would understand that.

Aggravating circumstances? Listen to yourself, Mr. Deligne! Anyone would think I've committed a crime. Are you *my* lawyer or my wife's?

Yes, the family law judge, I know. But there are no extenuating circumstances that would hold up in court. There are just the circumstances of love, that's all. And they're more on the attenuating side, at the end of the day. We got here by chance. I could have met Katia anywhere: at the supermarket, at the local coffeehouse, in one of my theater studies courses. But no: I met her because she came to live with us after her parents died in a car crash. I didn't jump on her, if that's what the judge wants to know. We talked a lot, we got to know each other, and we loved each other. It's completely natural. She's twenty-five years younger than me, okay. So what? Just like Woody Allen, and in his case it was his wife's adoptive daughter!

Legally, I'm not her uncle, not at all! Ask her whether she thinks of me as her uncle, ask Katia! When she left for Rodez (my wife found her a job, she agreed to go, you see, she tried to fight this), she was totally depressed, she was all alone, still grieving for her parents, and crazy about me. We talked every day on Skype or Facebook when my mother, uh, when my wife—ouch, sorry, spot the Freudian slip—when my wife wasn't around. Katia was afraid of my wife, she's her aunt but Katia felt she was hostile toward her happiness, and it's true that Claire really is very neurotic, what happened next proved that. She wasn't kind to Katia, she just wanted to get her out, get her away from the house, even though she had a sort of obligation to look after her.

Yes, probably. But it was too late anyway. Eventually you have to accept the facts. Acknowledge that you're wrong. I love Katia and I no longer love Claire. I want to divorce her and marry Katia.

The kids? I talked to the kids, you know. What they want is for everything to be okay. They really like Katia—excuse me? Yes, she's their cousin, so what? At least she's young, she understands them. A divorce would be best for everyone. It wouldn't stop them from loving their mother. And if she ever comes out, we could arrange joint custody. That would definitely be better for them than having to—being forced to—go see her in the psychiatric hospital.

So this is exactly the point I wanted to make. Claire's lawyer has put it to the family law judge that, because Claire is sick, it's wrong for me to ask for a divorce—apparently it's the "moral aspect of the marriage contract." Well, what I think is they're trying to extract as much money from me as possible, they want to claim damages and interest, and because I don't have the funds, they're using that to hold up the divorce. But this has nothing to do with any so-called illness. Claire isn't sick, she doesn't have cancer, as far as I know. She's not crazy either—that would have shown up, in all this time. Everyone can have episodes of hysteria. Panic attacks, blackouts, nervous breakdowns, we all get those. But she's gilding the lily. She was an actress, let's not forget that, she knows how to play it up.

Yes, but she's pretending, I'm killing myself here trying to get you to see that! I could do it too, couldn't I, wander through the streets naked saying people want to kill me, and I'm being persecuted. No, she's just sick with jealousy, crazy for what she's lost. I don't want to rub salt in the wound but her only illness is she's not aging well. And surely no one's going to stop me from getting a divorce because my wife has hormonal mood swings. I want to have a life, Katia wants kids...Can't she let us be happy for fuck's sake?

Yes, yes, I'll calm down.

I wouldn't have thought so. There are no damages, and the only vested interest is hers, because she wants to destroy me. Compensation, in a pinch. But compensation for what? She has a good job, friends, pastimes. She can have a perfectly good life without me, she could find a lover, especially if she stops dicking around like this, she could remarry, who knows? So I don't really see why I should give her money, honestly!

But let's get to why I'm here today. I brought a video of a documentary that was made at the La Forche Clinic, where my wife is...interned—well, they say "a resident," you know, the crazy, the depressed, the carers, the kitchen staff: they're all in the same boat. And I can tell you, you sometimes wonder who's who. The place is a shambles. Well anyway, a while ago, I told Chris—Christian Lantier, a video maker who worked on one of my shows—that he should do a piece on La Forche. He's basically a documentary maker, he immediately liked the idea, he wanted to work in a psychiatric environment, and he actually put a lot of himself into it, immersed himself, he must have had his own reasons. To make a long story short, he got the authorization he needed and did his filming last February. Okay, I won't show you all of it, you have other things to get on with, Mr. Deligne, but just watch this excerpt—wait, do you mind if I put it on your computer? Otherwise, I have it on my tablet, but it'll be smaller. So wait… [*click*] Skip this, skip this. Sequence two, here it is [*click*]. Oh actually, there's something else before that, this is interesting too [*click*]. They're reading a play, there are three of them, my wife Claire (the little blonde) and another chick she's very buddy-buddy with. And take a good look at the man, the young guy, watch how they look at each other, my wife and him.

ARAMINTE. *You shall find every consideration that is due to you here; and if at some later stage I have an opportunity to be of service to you, I shall not miss it.*

MARTON. *That is my lady: I recognize her.*

ARAMINTE. *It is true that it still angers me to see honest people with no fortune, when an infinite number of worthless people with no merit have dazzling wealth. It is a fact that pains me, especially in someone his age; because you must be only thirty at the very most?*

DORANTE. *Not quite yet, my lady.*

ARAMINTE. *What may be of some consolation to you is that you still have time to be happy.*

DORANTE. *I'm starting to be so today, my lady.*

[*click*] You get the picture. Really depressing, huh?…Yes, yes, of course, they're rehearsing, okay, but that's just the point: this is my line of work, Mr. Deligne, in case I have to remind you, I'm a theater director. I'm sure my wife's doing

it on purpose, she's taunting me. But [*click*] watch this bit, filmed in the gardens at La Forche, it's not very long.

[*Man's voice out of shot.*] Hi. Excuse me, could I interrupt for a moment? [*Collective nodding of heads: the same people as before.*] Today I'd like you to talk a little about yourselves, if you're okay with that. About life here. You, Claire, for example, how long have you been here? — I don't know exactly. Several springtimes. Several flowerbeds of daffodils. I must be in season three. How about you, Chris? — Um, me? — Yes, you. How long have you been here? — Well...I...[*he seems disconcerted*] — Chris, Chris. Do you know the story about the madman walking around the grounds of the asylum? No? So there's this madman walking around the grounds. He comes up to the boundary wall, climbs it, looks at the other side, and calls out to a passerby: "Hey, tell me, are there lots of you in there?" [*She gives a bright little laugh, the others laugh too.*]

[*click*] Right, stop, that's enough! Did you hear that, Mr. Deligne, did you hear the way she laughed? You can see she's perfectly fine. She's making fun of us, that's all, she's enjoying the trick she's playing on us. And at the taxpayer's expense, may I point out.

No, it's not worth it, the rest just gets worse and worse. Well, if you really want to...Let's drink the cup down to its last dregs. I warn you, she's always liked telling stupid jokes, like that, out of the blue, just as they come to her. She's no more crazy than you or I, and this is proof of it, she's acting, she's pretending so she can stay out of reach and keep the world at bay, that's all. And her literary quotations, her hodge-podge references, it's all the same. She's challenging us, me, Katia, but everyone else too. You, the judge, everybody.

[*click*]

Chris, Chris, film over there instead, film the park, film beauty and freedom. Do a big closeup of the daffodils, over there, did you see them? — [*A short balding man with a preoccupied expression comes over toward the group, waves hello to them, and, as he walks on past, says*] Lehem means bread. And also, something to warm you. And also, sex. — Thank you, Michel. [*Everyone in the group waves to say thank you.*] — Okay, Claire, I'll do that. But tell me, you didn't answer: don't you want to get out? Get back to your previous life, your work, your family? — Ah! Wait, I have another one, a really good one. There's a couple in their sixties, they've just retired and they're living a peaceful life in their little house. One day someone knocks at the door. There's an old lady on the doorstep and she asks for their help. They show her in and offer her a bed and some food. After she's eaten, she says, "My friends, I'm a fairy. You can each make a wish and I will make it come true to thank you for your kindness." They're thrilled, amazed, delighted. The woman goes first. "Well," she says, "because we retired recently and this is something we've always dreamed of, I'd like us to travel around the world together, a really beautiful long trip." "No problem," says the fairy. *Psshtt*. A cloud of gold dust, and suddenly the old lady has two tickets for a round-the-world cruise. "And you?" the fairy asks the husband. The man hesitates for a moment, looks sideways at his wife, bites his lip, then makes up his mind: "Listen, you're not going to like this but I'm sorry, I'll never have this opportunity again, so tough, here goes." He turns to the fairy and says, "I'd like to have a wife thirty years younger than me." "No problem," says the fairy. She waves her hand toward the husband and *psshtt*, he's ninety years old.

[*click*] Right, this time I'm stopping it. You see the sort of thing. And they're all laughing along with her, like a kids' playground. It drives me crazy, hearing her laugh.

The guy next to her? A psychiatrist, I think. Like I said, in that place you can't be too sure. He's her lover, most likely. Did you see the way they look at each other? They look real close, wouldn't you say? As thick as thieves, don't you think?

The other woman, the tall blonde with the piercing eyes? She kind of scares the shit out of me, that one. I don't really remember. Camille, um...Camille Morand, something like that. Apart from that, I don't really know, I think she's...Oh, yes I do! She's no one, she's a writer.

I dedicate this book to the memory of Nelly Arcan

Notes

Apart from the explicit references to various works, this novel contains reminiscences or quotations (some of them unfaithful) from A. Artaud, H. Melville, L. Aragon, J-F. Lyotard, N. Arcan, J. Racine, D. Winnicott, J. Didion, G. Flaubert, P. Lejeune, O. Steiner, J. Joyce, W. Shakespeare, J. Renard, M. Duras, P. Quignard, J. Lacan, W. B. Yeats, H. de Balzac, H. Cixous, R. M. Rilke, L-F. Céline, R. Juarroz, M. Leiris.

The poem quoted on p. 133 is by W. H. Auden.

The song "De la main gauche" (With my left hand) was written by Danielle Messisa.

The text on pp. 57–58 was loosely inspired by the work of J-P. Winter, *Les errants de la chair: Études sur l'hystérie masculine*, and various popular science Internet sites on the subject.

The words "People don't die, they're killed" (p. 56) is the leitmotif of a film whose title I've forgotten.

CAMILLE LAURENS is an award-winning French novelist and essayist. She received the Prix Femina, one of France's most prestigious literary prizes, in 2000 for *Dans ces bras-là*, which was published in the United States as *In His Arms* in 2004. She lives in Paris.

ADRIANA HUNTER has translated more than fifty books including Hervé Le Tellier's *Eléctrico W*, winner of the French-American Foundation's 2013 Translation Prize in Fiction. She won the 2011 Scott Moncrieff Prize, and her work has been short-listed twice for the Independent Foreign Fiction Prize. She lives in Norfolk, England.

⊞ OTHER PRESS

You might also enjoy these titles from our list:

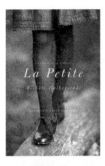

LA PETITE by Michèle Halberstadt

La Petite is neither grim nor sentimental. Every woman will recognize something of herself in this moving story about adolescent grief, solitude, and awakening.

"[A] touching glimpse of a young life nearly lost and then redeemed...[A] brief but powerful memoir...A haunting story with a triumphant conclusion." —*Kirkus*

COUPLE MECHANICS by Nelly Alard

At once sexy and feminist, this is a story of a woman who decides to fight for her marriage after her husband confesses to an affair with a notable politician.

"Nelly Alard delves into the core of infidelity with wry observation and subtlety. Riveting, beautifully detailed, and totally addictive. You won't be able to put this down." —Tatiana de Rosnay, *New York Times* best-selling author of *Sarah's Key*

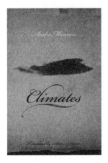

CLIMATES by André Maurois

First published in 1928, this magnificently written novel about a double conjugal failure is imbued with subtle yet profound psychological insights of a caliber that arguably rivals Tolstoy's.

"*Climates* is a delicious romantic bonbon that yanks the heartstrings." —*Wall Street Journal*

Also recommended:

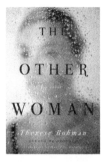

THE OTHER WOMAN by Therese Bohman

A psychological novel where questions of class, status, and ambition loom over a young woman's passionate love affair

"Bohman has a nose for danger: Her characters are curiously, alarmingly awake, and a story we should all know well is transformed into something wondrous and strange. A disturbing, unforgettable book." —Rufi Thorpe, author of *The Girls from Corona del Mar*

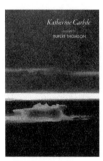

KATHERINE CARLYLE by Rupert Thomson

Unmoored by her mother's death, Katherine Carlyle abandons the set course of her life and starts out on a mysterious journey to the ends of the world.

"The strongest and most original novel I have read in a very long time...It's a masterpiece." —Philip Pullman, author of the best-selling His Dark Materials trilogy

ALL DAYS ARE NIGHT by Peter Stamm

A novel about survival, self-reliance, and art, by Peter Stamm, finalist for the 2013 Man Booker International Prize

"A postmodern riff on *The Magic Mountain*...a page-turner." —*The Atlantic*

"*All Days Are Night* air[s] the psychological implications of our beauty obsession and the insidious ways in which it can obscure selfhood." —*New Republic*